More acclaim for Kyoko Mori and *Shizuko's Daughter*

"BEAUTIFULLY WRITTEN ... Yuki's life is buoyed by the legacies that her mother bequeathed her: a love of art, nature and her aging grandparents. In the end, she forges a new life and even a sweet and happy romance."
—*Los Angeles Times Book Review*

"GRACEFUL ... Mori's beautiful and sensitive prose evokes a world of pungent memories.... A worthwhile novel about a resilient young woman's coming of age."
—*School Library Journal*

"STUNNING ... Mori paints beautiful pictures with words, creating visual images that can be as haunting and elliptical as poetry."
—*The Horn Book*

"[A] RARE ACHIEVEMENT ... A first novel that truly bridges the interests of young adults and adults, written in a spare, intricately balanced style ... Most impressive is Mori's flow of a narrative voice that subtly translates aesthetic observations into readers' experiences—the color and texture of flowers, of clothing, of pottery, of human love's pain and release.... Readers will feel enlightened."
—*The Bulletin of the Center for Children's Books*

By Kyoko Mori
Published by The Random House Publishing Group:

SHIZUKO'S DAUGHTER
ONE BIRD

SHIZUKO'S DAUGHTER

Kyoko Mori

BALLANTINE BOOKS • NEW YORK

RLI: $\underline{\text{VL: 5 & up}}$
IL: 6 & up

A Ballantine Book
Published by The Random House Publishing Group
Copyright © 1993 by Kyoko Mori

Published in the United States by Ballantine Books, an imprint of The Random House Publishing Group, a division of Random House, Inc., New York, and simultaneously in Canada by Random House of Canada Limited, Toronto.

Ballantine and colophon are registered trademarks of Random House, Inc.

www.ballantinebooks.com

Library of Congress Catalog Card Number: 92-26956

ISBN 0-449-70433-5

This edition published by arrangement with Henry Holt and Company, Inc.

Manufactured in the United States of America

First Ballantine Books Edition: June 1994

OPM 20 19 18 17

In memory of two grandmothers,
Fuku Nagai and Alice Brock

Contents

1
Housebound
(March 1969)

The village carpenter was standing on the bare rafters and throwing pink and white rice cakes to the crowd below. Shizuko lay on the couch in her living room in Kobe and dreamed that she was among the village children in red and blue kimonos chasing the hard, dry rice cakes that came down, like colored pebbles, from the sky. In the village where she was born, that was how people had celebrated the building of a new house. *It was difficult to catch the cakes in midair. Shizuko stopped. She picked the cakes off the ground before the others trampled on them and wrapped them in her white handkerchief to take home for her mother to wash and toast over the fire. The other children were still running around. Shizuko noticed that they were not the children she had played with before the War, but her daughter Yuki's school friends. But where is Yuki? Shizuko wondered. She is not here because I am. She can't come until I am gone. The next moment, the house and the children had vanished. Shizuko was in a park. She was watching Yuki chasing the white cherry blossom petals that were blowing about in the wind. They were coming down like confetti. Yuki ran around and around the tree in her pink spring dress and caught the*

1

*petals in midair. If she's not careful, Shizuko thought,
she will fall. Shizuko tried to call her, but her voice
would not come. Yuki continued to run in circles around
the cherry tree.*

The telephone was ringing in the hallway. Shizuko
woke up and pushed aside her blanket. As she got up
from the couch and walked slowly toward the noise, she
thought: In a month, the cherry trees will be in blossom.
It was strange to think that. Spring was late this year;
the first week of March had been gray and damp. I
won't be here to see, she thought. I wonder if the dead
can see or smell the flowers. She thought of how her
mother put fresh flowers on the Buddhist altar every
week in memory of her son who had been killed in the
War.

"Mama, can you hear me?" Yuki's voice sounded
anxious on the other end as Shizuko picked up the receiver. In the background, a stereo was playing a sym-
phony. "I'm calling from Miss Uozumi's house."

"What happened to your piano lesson?" Shizuko
asked. "I thought you were supposed to be taking it
now." She blinked and tried to clear her head. She was
still thinking of Yuki running around the cherry tree in
her dream.

"That's what I'm calling about," Yuki said. "Miss
Uozumi's going to be about an hour late. Her mother let
me in and gave me some tea. Miss Uozumi told her to
have me wait. Is that all right?"

"That's fine," Shizuko said.

"I won't be home until five or five thirty, just in time
for supper. Are you sure it's all right?"

"Of course," Shizuko said. "How was school?" She

2

knew she was stalling. Let me hear her voice just a while longer, she thought. I can't let her go. Not yet.

"So-so," Yuki said. "I scored two runs in baseball. Two of the boys on the other team said I bragged about it, so I had a fight with them during lunch break. Don't worry, Mama. Nobody was really hurt, and the teacher didn't scold anyone. I scraped my knee a little when I fell down, but I punched one of them, right in the stomach. I was winning before the teacher came and stopped us. You're not worried, are you? I'm not hurt, really."

"You should be careful, Yuki," Shizuko said, remembering her dream. "You may get hurt someday."

"I don't think so. Most of the kids won't fight me anymore. They're afraid of me."

"Be careful all the same."

"Sure," Yuki said. "What are you going to do this afternoon? You sound kind of tired. Are you all right?"

"I just woke up from a nap."

"I didn't mean to wake you up. Do you want to go back to sleep?"

"No," Shizuko said. "I'm awake now."

Yuki seemed to hesitate. "You're sure you don't want me to come right away? I can fix supper."

"No," Shizuko said. "You should wait for your lesson. You prepared for it all week."

"But I can practice the same pieces another week. I'm sure Miss Uozumi won't mind. She's always telling me to practice more. I'll tell her mother I have to go home."

"Don't do that," Shizuko said. "I'm only tired. You'd better go now."

"All right. I'll come home as soon as I'm done. Maybe we can eat out—then you won't have to cook.

I'm sure Father won't come home for supper. Can we go out to eat?"

"Maybe," Shizuko said. Her own voice sounded strange. She wondered if Yuki could hear it. "Yuki," she said. "Be good. You know I love you."

"I love you too, Mama. I'll see you later."

Shizuko held the receiver for a moment and waited for Yuki to hang up. When the click did not come, she hesitated for another moment and then put down the receiver. She pictured Yuki waiting on the other end for her to hang up first, her face puzzled and uncertain.

Shizuko went to the den, where she kept her sewing machine, ironing board, knitting basket, and a small desk for writing letters and taking care of the bills. Perhaps I haven't done so badly, she told herself as she thought of her fifteen years of marriage. Then she saw the cloth she had cut out for Yuki's new skirt and pinned to the sewing board. Triangular pieces of white cotton and maroon trimming, they reminded her of butterfly wings. She had meant to finish the skirt. But it was nearly three now; there was just enough time to write two notes—one for her husband, Hideki, and one for Yuki.

Somebody else will finish the skirt for her, Shizuko thought as she sat down at the desk and picked up her pen. She looked at the pad of blank paper and tried to concentrate. There was so much she had planned to do—she had even meant to clean out her closet and drawers, throw away some things and pack the rest to be saved for Yuki or given away to relatives. She had wanted to spare the others the trouble, the unpleasantness. She remembered the rainy morning after her mother-in-law's death, two years earlier. Her father-in-

4

law and her husband had left her and Yuki, only ten at the time, to dispose of the clothes and jewelry and books. "This is an awful thing to have to do," Yuki had said as she poured mothballs into a box of clothes to be given away to charity. "Why don't *they* help?" "It's women's work," Shizuko had told her. It's always women's work, she thought now as she sat at the desk with a sheet of blank paper, to deal with the consequences of other people's deaths, their mistakes, broken promises.

She did not know how to begin her note for Hideki. She thought of how she had wasted the day trying to put her things in order. In the end, she had given up. Unable to continue with her packing, she had moved about the house, straightening the vases and pictures in the living room, cleaning the windows in the kitchen, polishing the mirror in her room—all aimless tasks now—until she had lain down on the couch under the blanket and fallen asleep. Even that had seemed aimless, her need for temporary rest, when rest was all that was before her. And now, it was past three and she had barely enough time to write the two notes.

Please forgive me, she started to write in large, bold letters, *for my weakness, for the trouble I have caused you.* As I have forgiven your coldness, she thought, all the hours and days you were too busy to spare for Yuki and me, even the nights you have spent with another woman. These things I have forgiven, have had to forgive. *I do not do this rashly,* she continued, *but after much consideration. This is best for all of us. Please do not feel guilty in any way. What has happened is entirely my responsibility. This is the best for myself as well as for you. I am almost happy at this last hour and wish you to be.*

She signed the note and took out another sheet of paper. She knew what she wanted to tell Yuki. *In spite of this,* she wrote, *please believe that I love you. People will tell you that I've done this because I did not love you. Don't listen to them. When you grow up to be a strong woman, you will know that this was for the best. My only concern now is that you will be the first to find me. I'm sorry. Call your father at work and let him take care of everything.* Shizuko stopped to read over what she had written. This is the best I can do for her, she thought, to leave her and save her from my unhappiness, from growing up to be like me. Yuki had so much to look forward to. At twelve, she was easily the brightest in her class; all her teachers said so. The art teacher had been particularly impressed by her watercolors. They reflected, he said, her bold intelligence and imagination as well as her skills. *You are a strong person,* Shizuko continued. *You will no doubt get over this and be a brilliant woman. Don't let me stop or delay you. I love you.* As she signed the note, Shizuko pictured Yuki running to her in her new skirt, the white cotton and the maroon trimmings fluttering in the spring breeze like the sail of a new ship. Only, I won't be there to catch you, she thought, but you will do fine by yourself. You will be all right.

It was nearly four o'clock. I must hurry now, Shizuko thought. She walked to the kitchen, closed the door behind her, and laid the two notes on the table. Through the clear windows above the sink, she could see the fir trees in the backyard. Their dark foliage loomed against the damp gray sky.

She hesitated a second before she turned on the gas. No, she told herself as she turned it on. There's nothing

6

I've left undone that can be done now, there is nothing now, and I must sit down. She sat on the floor, with the table and chair legs rising above her head, and thought, This must be how the world looks to children, huge shapes, and lines going nowhere. The gas smelled almost sweet, but it was a foul sort of sweetness. The smell reminded her of the tiny yellow flowering weeds that had grown near her parents' house, on her way to school. The flowers, shaped like little stars, had smelled foul and sweet. She could not remember what they were called. In the fall, they would turn into white fuzz that flew about and got caught in her hair.

"I am almost happy at this last hour," she repeated the last words of her note to her husband, "and I wish you to be." No, she thought, suddenly springing up to her feet. I cannot say that. That is a lie. I cannot, must not, tell a lie now. She was dizzy. She groped for the notes on the table—it was hard to tell which was which now—found the right one, and sat back on the floor with it in her hand.

She could scarcely breathe. I can't light a match now, she thought. Shizuko held the note near her face for another moment, making sure that it was the one she wanted, and then tore it into tiny bits. Sick for breath, she tossed up the bits of paper and watched them come down like confetti, like the white petals of cherry blossoms, and rice cakes falling from the rafters midway to the sky, before she gave herself up to the near-approaching darkness.

2
The Wake
(March 1969)

The men were rearranging the living room for the wake. Upstairs, her aunt Aya, just arrived on the afternoon southbound train from Tokyo, began to put the clothes into wooden storage boxes for the attic. Yuki took down her mother's blue housecoat from the bathroom door and brought it to her aunt. A whole day had passed since her mother's death. Her father had not touched a single thing that had belonged to her mother, as though he thought of death as contagious.

Aya took the housecoat from Yuki and put it away. "You can wear some of these when you grow up," she said, her hand sweeping over the clothes inside the box.

Yuki sat down and watched as her aunt went back to the open closet. It was already half empty. Aya continued to take the remaining blouses and dresses off the hangers, fold them, and lay them inside the boxes. Off the hangers, the clothes suddenly collapsed and hung limp from Aya's hands. Yuki breathed in the faint smell of sawdust from the boxes. The soft silks and cottons Aya was putting away still smelled of her mother. They were mostly shades of green and blue. Soon, the closet was empty and the boxes were full. Her aunt poured out a handful of mothballs into each box and closed the lid on her mother's colors. Yuki imagined the smell of mothballs and dust filtering through them in the dark.

Aya shut the closet door and went to the bureau. From the top drawers, she pulled out a handful of silk scarves and jewelry and turned back to Yuki. "You've been so good," she said. "At your age, it must be so difficult."

Yuki looked away and at the photograph on the wall. On its glass frame the late-afternoon sun cast weak shadows of the fir trees outside, their branches swaying now and then in the breeze. It was like a double exposure: the moving branches outside superimposed on the still photograph of her family three or four years ago. In the photograph her mother stood between Yuki and her father, one hand on his arm and the other on Yuki's shoulder.

"Nobody would think you were only twelve," Aya said. "The way you've been acting, with such composure." She began to fold the scarves and stack them up on a pile of small articles to be distributed among friends and relatives as keepsakes. "You didn't even cry once."

Yuki was sick of such remarks: "You've been so good," "You're only twelve," "So brave." It seemed as though no one had said anything else to her since late yesterday afternoon, when, coming home from her piano lesson, she had found her mother unconscious on the kitchen floor.

She had dropped her books, turned off the gas, and called her father at work. He had told her not to call an ambulance and create a commotion—he would fetch a doctor himself and come home immediately. While she waited for them, Yuki opened the windows to let out the gas. Then she sat down and touched her mother's forehead. It felt surprisingly cool. The air from the windows might be too cold, she thought. She went and lowered the windows. Her mother was no longer breathing, and Yuki was not sure exactly when her breath had stopped. Now, a day later, the smell of gas seemed to cling to Yuki's clothes, her hair. She washed her hair over and over to get it out, but it lingered.

After the doctor had said that there was no hope, Yuki walked into the den and found the white cotton and maroon trimmings cut out for her new skirt and laid out on the sewing board. The triangular pieces, with silver tacks scattered over them, looked like the remnants of a shipwreck. And Yuki thought: When did you decide to do it? Just this morning you were trying to sew.

Even then, she didn't cry. She picked up her mother's address book from the desk and went to the hallway to phone her relatives and friends, absentmindedly staring at her mother's handwriting, while her father was in the kitchen with two policemen who had been called by the doctor.

The sound of the jangling metal made Yuki look up. Her aunt was now going through the jewelry and cosmetics left in the other drawers. They went in two piles, to be saved or discarded. Most of the jewelry would be saved, except for bracelets whose clasps no longer fastened, odd earrings that did not match, all the small broken things her mother had kept. The cosmetics would be discarded. As Aya swept a handful of lipstick and eye shadow off the pile into the wastebasket, one roll of lipstick slipped through her fingers and fell on the floor. The cap came off and the lipstick rolled to the edge of the carpet.

"Your poor mother," Aya said. She turned aside and pressed her fingers to her eyes.

Yuki picked up the lipstick. Its tip, cut at a sixty-degree angle, had scarcely been blunted. She put the cap back on and dropped the roll in the wastebasket, thinking of how the lipstick, too, smelled of her mother.

She had not been downstairs since the early afternoon. Yuki stood at the door of the living room, unable to go in. The room looked completely unfamiliar. She couldn't believe it was the same room where she and her mother had sat listening to music or drawing together, drinking tea after dinner and talking. Yuki stared silently at the makeshift altar, the coffin in the center, the white and yellow chrysanthemums drenched in the smoke from the incense sticks. White drapery was everywhere, covering the floor and the walls in large, billowy folds. Yuki tried to remember where each piece of furniture had been: the armchair where her mother had sat, the glass table on which they had put their cups of tea and plates of cake, the footstool where she had sat, always close enough to reach over and hand her mother a drawing to look at or a book to read, the piano she had played while her mother closed her eyes, listening. All these things had been moved out of the room or shoved behind the drapery.

A man in a black suit passed by her and joined the small group of mourners who sat on the floor, almost swallowed up by the immense whiteness. Their backs were toward Yuki. Among them, she saw her grandparents, who had come up from the countryside during the night. Her grandmother's back was bent more than usual, as though she were crouching from pain. "It's

11

cruel," she had said in the morning when she came into the kitchen, where Yuki was washing her hair in the sink. "I never wanted to live and see my own daughter's death. I thought all my children would outlive me a long time."

Aya had come out of the kitchen and was standing next to Yuki. "Don't you have anything darker to wear?" she whispered.

"I don't know," Yuki said. She looked at her pale blue dress and remembered how she and her mother had chosen the handwoven material at a craft fair in Kyoto, the same day they had bought a tea set the color of ripe persimmons. "You wanted me to wear blue or gray if I didn't have anything in black," she said.

"I meant dark blue," Aya said.

"You didn't say."

"Let's go back to your room and find something more appropriate."

Yuki followed her aunt up the stairs. The priest was just arriving. From the stairway landing, she saw him coming into the house with her father. The priest's black robe ballooned around him and made him look like a buoy riding on the sea. Yuki thought of the musty smells of old cloth, temple burying grounds in the rain. Her father did not look up; he did not notice her standing on the landing. They had scarcely talked since yesterday afternoon when he had told her not to call an ambulance. The doctor he'd brought took one look at her mother and shook his head. It was too late, the doctor said, her mother wasn't breathing. Yuki tried again to think back to the moment when she had come into the kitchen and found her mother on the floor. No matter how hard she tried, the only thing she was sure of was that her mother's forehead had been not exactly cold, but not warm anymore after she had opened the windows. Exactly when did she stop breathing? Yuki wondered. Why didn't I check her breath right away?

Her aunt was waiting. Yuki turned the corner and stepped into her bedroom, across the landing from her mother's room, where she and her aunt had put away the clothes in the afternoon.

Aya closed the door behind them and motioned for Yuki to turn around. Yuki stood still and felt Aya's fingers down her back, her forefinger drawing a strong straight line, peeling open the zipper. Yuki stepped out of the dress and sat on the edge of her bed in her white slip while Aya hung up the dress in the closet and quickly examined the other clothes. The hangers squeaked on the metal pole and rattled against one another. Yuki listened to the dry, hollow sounds.

Her throat tightened. There was something utterly humiliating about sitting on the bed nearly naked while her aunt went through her clothes, moving the hangers and opening and shutting the drawers, just as she had gone through her mother's clothes. Maybe I'll die too, Yuki thought, and Aunt Aya will pack my clothes just like she did Mama's. She imagined her clothes folded and crammed inside a wooden box, her scarves and handkerchiefs stacked up in a limp pile to be discarded or given away. Her chest felt as though something sharp was stuck inside.

Aya laid out a white blouse and a gray jumpskirt on the bed. "There. You'd better hurry now. The wake will be starting in a few minutes."

Yuki sat fingering the hem of the gray jumpskirt. That was the only thing she had in a dark color—part of

13

her school choir outfit. She and her mother had laughed at its ugliness, its drab shapelessness. Yuki watched her aunt close the door on a closetful of brilliant colors, the clothes her mother had made for her. But she's dead now, and they want me to wear my ugly choir outfit, she thought; maybe they'll want me to sing, too.

"Shall I stay and help you?" Aya asked.

Yuki shook her head.

"I'll see your downstairs then. Hurry."

Aya left the room. Yuki sat and listened to her steps down the staircase. When she couldn't hear them anymore, she took a deep breath. As she exhaled, the tears she had been holding back began to come out of her eyes. She blinked hard and wiped her face on the pillow. She put her arms through the blouse. From downstairs, the brass bell sounded and the priest's chanting began. It was interrupted occasionally by the mourners responding in chorus. Their words were inaudible, just a wailing monotone. Yuki finished buttoning the blouse, stood, and stepped into the jumpskirt; but when she pulled it up, she couldn't bear to zip it—her fingers went cold when she reached in the back, and she wanted to cry again. The wailing continued from below.

Yuki dropped the skirt on the floor and walked to the closet. She pulled open the door and turned on the light switch. The bright colors of her clothes flooded the small, square space. She closed the door behind her and sat on the floor of her closet, her cheeks touching the soft hems of her summer dresses. She pulled her knees up against her chest and covered her ears with cupped hands. Then she looked up and breathed in the colors. She would drown out the wailing chant with their brilliance.

3
Tiptoes
(April 1970)

Her father's new bride had been in the dressing room for nearly three hours. Yuki stopped outside the door and tried to steady herself. She couldn't get over the feeling that the floor underneath her was still rocking. She had arrived on the morning train from Tokyo, where she had been living with her aunt Aya since her mother's death a year earlier. Aya had come with her and was waiting in the coffee shop downstairs.

Yuki hesitated a moment with her hand on the door-knob. She could still taste the sourness of the tangerines she had eaten on the train. She pushed open the door and walked straight toward the window without looking at anything else. The dressing room was on the fifth floor of the hotel where the wedding would take place; from the window, she could see the port of Kobe only six or seven blocks to the south. The early afternoon sunlight cast a sheen on the calm water.

Slowly, Yuki turned toward the bride, who sat in front of the mirror along one of the walls. She had already put on several layers of the wedding kimono—everything but the silver-white outermost layer, which hung on the wooden rack on the opposite wall. The clothes she had worn to the hotel—a brown knit dress,

15

coffee-colored nylons, and black high heels—lay in a heap on a folding chair in the corner. Her hair was pulled back, her head covered with a white towel, and two women from a beauty salon were massaging her face and neck with glossy white face cream.

"Aunt Aya said that I should come and see you," Yuki said to the bride. "She said you'd probably want to talk to me before the ceremony."

The beauty salon women stopped massaging the bride's face and began to wash their hands in the sink by the mirror.

"You've never seen anyone getting dressed for a wedding, have you?" the bride said. "Why don't you stay and watch me for a while? It's all us girls in here, you see. No man, not even your father, is allowed to see me until I come into the ceremony."

"Father won't miss it," Yuki said. "He doesn't care that much about clothes and makeup. He used to tell Mama that she made me too many clothes. He said people shouldn't care too much about their appearances. He'd be bored watching people get dressed for three hours." Yuki put her hand on the window ledge. She felt dizzy. The metal on the ledge was surprisingly cold.

"You were very fond of your mother, weren't you?" the bride said. Yuki remained silent. *In spite of this,* her mother had written in the note she had left on the kitchen table, *please believe that I love you.*

"There shouldn't be any hard feelings between us," the bride was saying. She lifted her long, thin hand to her temple and pushed a stray wisp of her hair back under the towel. Her fingers looked bony and her nails were painted silver. "You'll probably hear people say all kinds of bad things about me because I was married to your father so soon after your mother's tragic death. They may even say that I've always had my eye on him—that I drove your mother to her death. You know how people talk."

People will tell you that I've done this because I did not love you, her mother had written. *Don't listen to them.*

"You shouldn't believe what they say," the bride said. "I've known your father for a long time because we worked in the same office. But there was nothing between us, and there's no reason for you to be angry at us. I want all of us to be happy together. Do you understand?"

From the window, Yuki counted the ships in anchor. There were six on the south pier. She remembered the first time her mother had taken her to the port to see the ships. All the way down the pier, Yuki had kept asking, "What are those tall buildings? What are they doing in the water?" At the end of the pier, with nothing between her and the large black and gray shapes but ten yards of shiny water surface, Yuki had realized that these were the very ships she had come to see. They looked nothing like the ships in her picture books, which were colorful triangles and rectangles stacked up together with a single column of smoke coming out at the top. *You will no doubt get over this and be a brilliant woman,* her mother had written. *Don't let me stop or delay you.* I'll never get over it, Mama, Yuki thought.

"Are you listening to me, Yuki?" the bride said. The beauty salon women began to dab her face with cotton squares drenched in flesh-colored paint. When they were done, the bride's face and chin were a shade lighter than her neck. Although she was several years

17

younger than Yuki's mother had been, her skin was tired looking where there was no makeup. Yuki remembered the first time her father had come up to Tokyo with her; that was eight months ago. He had telephoned the night before and said that he was bringing a very pretty woman with large pretty eyes who wanted so much to be Yuki's friend.

"Of course I'm listening," Yuki said. She looked away from the window and at the silver-white kimono on the rack, its large sleeves spread out like the wings of a huge bird.

"Will you call me Mother?"

"Yes," Yuki said. "Mother. But not Mama, like I called my own mama. May I go now?"

"We'll be happy together, won't we? And you'll try to like me?"

"I can't promise you that," Yuki said. "I mean about being happy. I don't think I'll be happy." She felt a lump in her throat. The air was heavy with the perfumes of hair oils and makeup. "I have to go. I can't stand the smell of makeup. I'll be sick if I stay." She turned away from the window and ran out of the room.

She ran down the hallway and through the door that led to the stairs. The red wool dress she was wearing made her neck and legs itch. Her father and the bride had bought the dress for her when they had been in Tokyo the second and last time to visit her. "Make sure you wear it to the wedding," her father had said. Yuki ran down the first flight of stairs and jumped down the last three steps. She held on tighter to her white bead purse as she continued to run. Her mother had made it for her a long time ago. Nobody had objected to her carrying it to the wedding—her father probably didn't even remember who had made it. He had met her and Aya at the train station and taken them out to breakfast. Nobody had said much, and he had kept looking at his watch. Then he left, saying that he needed to take care of some last-minute things, and Yuki went with her aunt to check into the hotel room where they were to spend the night. In the morning, her aunt would leave for Tokyo and her father and his bride would meet her in the lobby and take her back home. Yuki hadn't been to the house since her mother's death. She didn't want to go back.

After the second flight of stairs, Yuki slowed down to a walk and clasped the purse against her chest. Inside the purse, she was carrying a small picture from her mother's wedding. It was one of her favorite pictures of her mother; she could see everything without actually looking at the picture. Her father and mother were standing in front of the main gate of a temple in Kyoto. Her mother had her hand on her father's forearm and was leaning toward him. "If you look carefully," she had told Yuki once, "you can tell I was standing on tiptoes and leaning on your father's arm. The dress I rented turned out to be too long for me, and I didn't want the hem to drag in the picture. I couldn't do anything else about it at the last minute. We didn't have a lot of money then. We got married Western-style because the rentals were so much cheaper that way."

When she got to the first floor, Yuki walked to another wing of the hotel, where the coffee shop was. The shop was almost empty. Among the white tables and chairs and potted plants with shiny leaves like little palm trees, she could see her aunt Aya sitting by the window. Yuki went to the table and pulled out the chair opposite her. From the window, she could see the tall white buildings of downtown Kobe and the mountains to the north. The sea was on the other side.

"I ran out on her," Yuki said as she sat down. She set her purse on the empty chair next to her.

Aya put down her coffee. She was wearing a peacock-blue suit, very much like the suit Yuki's mother used to wear to concerts and plays. Aya was two years younger than Shizuko and just a little taller; they had the same light brown eyes and large hands with broad palms.

"Why did you do that?" Aya's voice sounded more tired than angry.

"She wanted me to watch her get dressed and have her face done. It was embarrassing. Her other clothes were all over the chair." Yuki rested her eyes on her aunt's hands on the table. Finally, the rocking of the floor was going away. "Do you know what I have in my purse? A picture of Mama's wedding. Do you want to see it?"

"Yuki, please don't make this more difficult than it is."

"I want to hear again about when Mama was young, about how she wouldn't marry the rich man Grandma wanted her to marry. Will you tell me about it again?"

"I don't know," Aya said. "This isn't a very good time for that story. I wish you wouldn't be so difficult."

"If you tell me the story again, I'll behave better for the rest of the day."

"Will you? You won't make a fuss during the ceremony? You'll sit quietly and not talk, or stand up when you're supposed to be sitting?"

"I promise I'll be good. But you have to tell me the

20

story nicely. Don't skip anything. Tell me nice and slow, the way Mama told stories."

"All right, but you must keep your word now." Aya leaned forward and sighed. "As you know, this all happened the year after the War, when we lived in the village where your grandma and grandpa are still living. Until that year, our family had been landowners in the village, as far back as anyone could remember. But the land reform had begun. The government people came and made us sell most of our land for next to nothing, to give it to our tenant farmers. You've studied this part at school. Maybe it was a good thing for many people, but it wasn't for us. We were suddenly very poor. Our oldest brother had been killed in the War, and some of us were too young to be much help to our parents.

"Your grandma, though, wasn't completely discouraged. Your mother was now the oldest of us five children and she was seventeen, a good age to marry. So your grandma wanted her to marry the son of the richest family in the next village. She and Grandpa made an arrangement with the man's parents, who said they would be delighted to have such a good daughter-in-law. This family, too, had been landowners, but most of their land was up in the mountains. It was timberland, so they weren't required to sell. The government wanted only the rice paddies. Still, the man's parents thought that landowning families should stick together and help each other. They gave our family some gifts to celebrate the engagement—a white ceramic vase and landscape paintings—and set the date for the wedding. Then Grandma went home and told your mother that she had arranged a splendid match for her. Your mother was furious. She hadn't been told anything in advance.

21

Grandma was furious also, and she said to your mother, 'I've found such a nice match for you, and this is the thanks I get for it? If you really don't want to marry the young man, you will have to take these gifts back yourself and tell his family about it. I'm not going to do it for you.' Grandma never thought she would actually do it. But the next morning, your mother got up early before anyone else was awake to stop her, walked to the landowner's house, returned the gifts, and told them that if she ever wanted to get married, she would find her own husband."

Aya took a sip of her coffee and continued, "Later on, your mother told me that she had scarcely slept the night before she took back the gifts. She worried all night, thinking maybe she should accept the match to help us all. But how could she spend her life with a man she had never met? She could never love him. She would be so unhappy. She couldn't make a sacrifice like that, because she would live to resent it and turn into a bitter person. So she promised herself that she would work hard and help us in every other way, but not by accepting the match." Aya stopped.

"That's why my mother came to Kobe to work," Yuki said. "She couldn't stay in the village after the news got out about her outrageous behavior. In Kobe, she worked as a secretary for two years. She lived in a little attic room without heat because she was sending home most of her money. Then eventually, she met Father."

"Yes," Aya said.

"And Father had tuberculosis and Mama was at the hospital every day with him for a year until he was well again. She didn't give him up even when people said that he was going to die anyway and she was making a

22

fool of herself. She wouldn't leave him because they were engaged and she loved him."

Aya was silent.

"After all that," Yuki said, "how can Father marry someone else in a year? It isn't fair. And she's such a ninny."

"You shouldn't say things like that," Aya said.

"But she is," Yuki insisted. "She wanted us to be *happy*. She wanted me to watch her get dressed because we were all *girls* together." She took a sip from her aunt's untouched water glass. The water was lukewarm. "After all, you didn't get married when Uncle died. I heard you tell Mama that you couldn't even think of such a thing."

"It's different for men," Aya said. "They need someone to take care of the house and their children."

Neither spoke for a while. Then Aya said, "After this, you won't see me very often anymore. Your things should arrive on the truck next week."

Yuki said nothing.

"You must understand how awkward it would be otherwise," Aya said. "She has her own relatives, who will become your relatives. You'll see me and Grandpa and Grandma on special occasions, of course."

"Like funerals," Yuki said.

"Don't be that way," Aya said. "Can't you see it can't be helped? You are your father's only child. We have no claim on you. It was kind enough of your father to invite me to the wedding."

"You know it's a lie," Yuki said. "It's all a lie, the whole thing. They know I want to stay in Tokyo with you, and they'd like it that way too. They don't care about me. They only came to see me twice the whole

23

time I was with you. They'd as soon be by themselves. Only they won't do it because it would look bad. People would talk."

Yuki looked out the window. She could see the concert hall where she had performed in her first piano recital when she was six. After she played her two pieces, she went out to the stairway landing outside to get fresh air and look at the ships. Her mother slipped out the other door and went to buy her a bouquet of pink roses. Yuki could still see her mother running up the stairway in her white dress, the roses a blur of pink and green. She had stood and hugged her mother, gingerly, with her back bent, so as not to crush the roses between them.

"I'll miss you, so much," Yuki said.

Yuki was seated between her aunt and an old friend of her father's, a man who had come to her mother's funeral. The ceremony would start in a few minutes, when the bride came in. Yuki looked around. The room was dimly lit with the long white candles on the altar in the front. The guests were all seated at the three long tables arranged in a horseshoe around the altar. About twenty men and women: the bride's relatives, Yuki's father's side of the family, a few business friends. The men were wearing dark-colored suits; most of the women wore formal black kimonos. The smell of old cloth and candles was suffocating. The room had no windows. Yuki longed for the hallway outside, the busy lobbies of the hotel, people with suitcases coming and going.

Her father was standing on the side of the altar, away from the door. In his black kimono, he looked small and old. He was not looking at anyone in particular around the table but seemed to be staring into the air about two feet above everybody's head. He reminded Yuki of an old man trying to remember something: the lines of a poem, a song he hadn't sung in years. The priest stood on the other side of the altar in his red-and-white ceremonial robe. He was holding a wand of green branches tied up with red-and-white paper. Yuki looked away from the priest and his wand, at her own hands under the table. She pressed them harder against her purse and tried to picture her parents standing in front of the temple gate. Through the open gate, in the background, she could imagine the green leaves of the trees in the temple garden. The wedding had taken place in May. She could almost smell the wisteria blossoms on the other side of the temple buildings, in the arbors near the pond. The breezes of May would carry their scent all the way to the temple gate. She looked again at her father standing in the middle of the horseshoe and thought: Can't you remember all that, the open air, the scent of flowers and green leaves, and her hand pressing against your arm?

The door opened and the bride entered. She walked slowly under her huge wig and layers of kimono. The people around the tables rose when the bride stopped between the priest and the groom.

Yuki stood up with the rest and put down her purse on her seat. Her father's friend's jacket sleeve brushed against her hand. She leaned closer to her aunt. The priest began to shake the wand over the couple and to chant. Yuki could not understand the words that he intoned in a high, nasal voice. She thought of another priest who chanted at her mother's funeral, how she

25

didn't understand him either. Let me sit down before the floor starts rocking again, she thought.

After the chant, the priest handed Yuki's father a large earthenware bowl of ceremonial sake. Yuki watched him drink the warm rice wine from the bowl three times and hand it to the bride. The bride drank from it. Then the priest passed the bowl to Yuki's table. Each person drank from it three times and passed it to the right. Yuki stood watching the bowl come down the table to Aya. Aya took it and tipped it toward her face. The bowl was so large it looked as though her face would be swallowed inside it. Aya lifted it away from her mouth and passed it to Yuki.

The bowl felt heavy in her hands. As she lifted it slowly toward her mouth, the pungent smell of sake made her want to cough. She closed her eyes tight against the smell. In a blur, she saw her mother standing in front of the temple gate in her white wedding dress among wisteria blossoms and the spring breeze, her body a soft weight against the black sleeve. Mama, I can't do it, she thought, I can't let him forget. She stood on her tiptoes and tilted the bowl toward her face. The sake trickled into her mouth, warm and bitter. She drank it down in one long draft. Then, while her father's friend reached out his black sleeves for the bowl, Yuki brought her heels down with all her weight, dropping the bowl and shattering it against the tabletop—just as, on the morning of the funeral, her father had shattered her mother's rice bowl against the doorsteps so her ghost would not haunt his household or anyone in it.

4
Irises
(April 1970)

Her father and stepmother were in their room watching an afternoon movie on television. Yuki could see them through the open door as she passed by. They sat side by side on their futon bedding, the TV flickering in front of them. Though it was sunny, they had closed the heavy, rust-colored curtains her stepmother had put up. Her father's room looked small and crowded with her stepmother's things: the TV, her clothes, her makeup stand and dresser, the new futon with a shiny pink cover. The upstairs room that used to be Yuki's mother's was stripped of its furniture and the curtains.

Neither her father nor stepmother looked up from the movie to notice her. Yuki went to the kitchen and opened the right-hand door of the cupboard. Her mother's heavy, blue-tinted glasses and white ceramic goblets were gone. Instead, there were stacks of white porcelain plates and saucers with tiny pink flowers on the rim. Matching cups hung from the hooks her father must have just screwed in. Yuki tried the left-hand door and found a few dozen glasses lined up in rows, upside down. They were clear, tall tumblers and small juice glasses, all of them new and fragile looking. On this shelf, her mother had stacked up ceramic plates with blue and purple glaze dipped down the middle, each pattern slightly different, like the phases of the moon.

Yuki opened the new yellow refrigerator, took out the orange juice, and poured it into one of the new tumblers. She stared at the persimmon-colored tea set inside the glass cabinet. It was the only thing that hadn't been changed in the kitchen. On the day she and her mother had bought the tea set at a craft fair, the potter who made it was working at his wheel. The clay rose up into a perfect cylinder as he treadled. He pinched the side and made it flare out like a large petal; then he took the finished vase off the wheel and examined its shape, frowning. Finally, he held it between the heels of his hands and pressed slowly, carefully, till the cylinder was slightly askew. "Why does he do that?" Yuki asked. "He doesn't want a perfect shape," her mother answered. "He wants it just a touch bent and imperfect." No two things should be exactly the same, her mother had taught her.

Carrying her orange juice, Yuki walked back past her father's room and up the stairs to hers. She closed the door. At least her room had remained the same: the pale blue curtains she and her mother had chosen, the desk her grandfather had made, the dresser, the bed with the red quilted cover from her grandmother. Yuki took a sip of her juice and sat down on the floor among the four boxes sent from Tokyo by her aunt Aya. Just that morning Yuki had opened them up and read the note packed on top of her summer clothes. *Yuki, I hope you are well,* Aya had written. *My house seems empty without you. You know that I miss you and think of you often. I understand how difficult this move is for you. Please be brave. Try to be happy where you are.*

Yuki put the note in her desk drawer and began to un-pack her clothes. As she hung up her dresses and skirts in the closet, folded the sweaters and put them in the drawers, she thought of another move. Just two years ago she and her mother had packed their things to move to this house.

That day, too, was a Saturday in early April. But it was raining rather than sunny. The cherry blossoms in the nearby park had opened the week before. Yuki was sorry about the rain. It was coming down with enough force to shatter the fragile cups of flowers. The bruised petals would scatter over the asphalt walkways, the blue swing set, the silver bowl of the drinking fountain.

Yuki and her mother had been packing all morning, each in her own room. By eleven, Yuki was almost done with her things. The movers were coming at three. All over the house, there were half-filled boxes, piles of jackets, books, magazines, bedsheets, and towels. They hadn't even started on the kitchen or the living room. Only her father's bedroom was already cleaned out. Before he left on his business trip a week earlier, he had packed his things and piled the boxes against the wall in the hallway. The boxes were marked, taped, neatly stacked up. He said he would come back to the new house on Sunday morning and unpack his things into his bedroom and his new study. Yuki knew he would be done in half a day, everything arranged perfect and or-derly, just in time for him to take off on another busi-ness trip. She scarcely ever saw him.

Yuki taped shut the last box in her room and went to the kitchen. She took the glasses and plates out of the cupboard and lined them up on the tiled floor. Then she sat down in her red T-shirt and blue jeans, a pile of old newspapers on her right side and the glasses on her left. She didn't mind this job. She was proud of how careful she could be. She crumpled the papers inside the glasses, wrapped each glass twice. The newspapers had pictures of politicians, movie stars, criminals and accident victims, newly married couples. Their faces got crumpled against the blue of the glasses. Yuki filled the box, taped it shut, and pushed it away. She reached out for the next box, ready to start on the plates.

"You're working very hard."

Yuki turned around toward the doorway. Her mother was standing there in her mint-green housedress, her hair pinned up into a bun. Yuki and her mother both had long hair. Yuki's came down to her waist, and her mother's to her shoulders. Yuki had pulled back hers into a ponytail to keep it out of her eyes.

"I'm almost done with the breakable things," she told her mother. "I'll throw the pots and pans into a few big boxes. We're not going far. We don't have to pack them that carefully, do we?"

"No," Shizuko said. "How ever you can pack them is fine."

The new house was two miles to the north. They would still be in Kobe, but living near the mountains rather than the sea. When the first term started in mid-April, Yuki would be going to a different school. Her mother had been worried all week about the school. She started talking about it again.

"You really don't mind going to the new school?" she asked Yuki. "Maybe I should see about keeping you at the old school for sixth grade. Next April might be a better time to change, when everyone has to start at the junior high school. You won't be the only one who's new. I can get permission from the school board for you to stay. But then you'd have to take the city bus every morning. I don't know."

Yuki sighed and shook her head so her mother would see how fed up she was. "I wish you wouldn't keep asking me the same thing. I already told you I don't mind. I'm not worried, so you should stop."

"But kids will pick on you at first, just because you're new."

"I don't care. I can take care of myself. I'm not afraid of anyone."

"When other kids tease you," her mother said, "you should ignore them. They'll give up sooner or later. You make things worse by getting upset. That's exactly what they're hoping you will do. You should pretend you didn't even hear them."

"Mama, you don't understand. I'm not going to let anyone make fun of me or say mean things to me and get away with it. But I don't want to talk about this anymore. I have a lot to do here. You're bothering me." She turned back to her packing and crumpled another newspaper.

Her mother sighed and went away. Yuki continued to pack the plates and then the large ceramic goblets, green soup bowls, and blue cups. She could remember where and when she and her mother had bought each ceramic piece: at craft fairs in Kyoto, in the old pottery villages north of Kobe. The best pottery, her mother said, was pottery you could use every day. Cups should feel solid in your hands and smooth against your lips. The glaze should be subtle rather than overbright. Bottoms of pieces were always plain. Potters scraped off any glaze that dripped there because in the kiln, glaze on the bottom would make the piece stick to the floor and crack. Her mother knew so much, Yuki thought. There wasn't much Yuki knew that she hadn't been taught by her mother. By the time she was done packing the breakable things, she felt bad about the way she had spoken.

She knew that her mother couldn't help being worried. Yuki had often gotten into trouble at school for fighting with the boys. Sometimes she came home with bruises or cuts. Last fall, she gave one boy a hairline fracture when she pushed him and he fell back against a stone wall, shoulder first. Her mother was called to school for that. "It could have been you with the broken shoulder," her mother said on the way home. "Promise me you'll stay out of trouble from now on." Yuki had tried to laugh it off. "I can't make a promise that I can't keep," she said. "Besides, his shoulder wasn't exactly broken. It was more like a small crack. And he started the fight by throwing my books into the puddle."

Yuki packed the utensils, pots, and pans into a few large boxes and went to her mother's room. Her mother was kneeling on the floor among piles of dresses, scarves, handkerchiefs, jewelry. She had only two boxes finished. Yuki went in and stood opposite her.

"I keep thinking I should look through these clothes first," her mother said. "Some of them are too bright for me now." She pointed at a white dress with teal-blue roses printed down the front. "That dress, for one."

"No," Yuki protested. "I like you in it."

Her mother shook her head. "It's time for me to start wearing more subdued colors. By the time my mother

32

was forty, she only wore ivory, light gray, and the darker blues."

"But Grandma's different," Yuki said, "and you're not forty yet."

"I will be this winter, and Grandma's not different. When I'm sixty, I'll be wearing grays and browns too, just like she does. All old women dress like that."

Yuki frowned. She couldn't imagine her mother being old like her grandmother, who had always been old as long as Yuki could remember.

"I wonder what it's like to be sixty," her mother said. "That's a long time to live."

Yuki sat down next to her on the floor. "I think you should wear everything you have," she said. "Besides, this isn't a good time to throw things out. You can always do that later. You know you'll have more time then."

Her mother laughed. "Yuki, you're so full of common sense."

Yuki leaned forward and cleared her throat. "I came to apologize," she said. "I spoke impertinently just a while ago. I'm sorry. I hope you're not mad at me."

"No, I'm not mad." Her mother rubbed Yuki's forehead with her fingertips. "There's a smudge on your forehead. It must be from the newspapers. I can't get it off."

"That's okay. I'll wash my face later."

Her mother said, "Remember when you ate the tube of my watercolor paint? It was yellow. Your mouth and chin were covered with it. I had to take you to the hospital. I was so worried."

Yuki recalled the bright yellow her mother had been using to paint lemon lilies. It was five or six years ago.

"I must have been five or six already, wasn't I? That was such a pretty color. I thought it would taste good. It tasted terrible. But I kept eating because I thought it would taste better once I got used to it. I was a dumb kid in a way."

Outside, the rain was turning into a drizzle. The sky was a lighter gray than it had been all morning. Yuki pulled her knees up to her chest and sat leaning forward, her arms draped around her legs.

"What will we do with our flowers?" she asked. "Are we going to dig them out and take them?"

"I don't know. Maybe we should leave them. Some of the perennials are ready to bud. This isn't a good time to move them. You're supposed to do that in the fall, when they're finished flowering."

"They might die if we don't take them. What if the new people don't know how to take care of them?"

"Do you want me to take them?"

"I think so. I'll miss them otherwise. They're our flowers."

"It isn't hard to get more. Your grandma can give us lots more."

"They won't be the same. I want these flowers." Yuki reached over for an empty box and began to put her mother's dresses inside it. "I'll take care of this if you want to go dig them out. I'd do it for you, but you're better at it. I don't want to hurt their roots."

"All right. We'll take them."

Her mother stood up to go. Yuki filled one box with the dresses and put the silk scarves on top. They were in shades of green and blue, some purple and dark pink.

"Your scarves are so pretty," she said.

Her mother stopped and looked back. "Someday

when I can't wear them anymore," she said, "maybe you'll be old enough to wear them for me."

"No," Yuki said. "I like them on you. I didn't mean that I wanted them."

"I know," her mother said, going out. Yuki hesitated a minute, looking up into the empty doorway. Then she went back to packing.

When Yuki finished filling the boxes, her mother was still outside. From the window, she could see her in the back of the garden in her black raincoat. Yuki took a red umbrella from the hallway and stepped outside. The rain was only a drizzle now, but it was chilly.

She went and stood next to her mother, who was digging some chrysanthemums with her hand spade and putting them into small planters. Gently but firmly Shizuko patted down the roots of each plant with her fingers. She already had a big box half filled with planters of chrysanthemums. Farther in the back, there were holes in the ground where the columbines and violas had been. Some violas were still left. These had started from the seeds off the larger plants the previous fall. They were too small to transplant. Yuki bent over them. She touched their wispy new leaves.

"Don't worry," her mother said. "Violas are hardy. Even if no one takes care of the yard, they'll bloom and multiply on their own, just like the violets near your grandparents' house. They're related, I told you, didn't I?"

Yuki imagined the violas blooming among weeds, their yellow-and-purple faces streaked with orange pollen. In the fall, their seeds would scatter like golden dust.

She walked back and crouched next to her mother, holding the umbrella over them both.

"I already have three boxes of columbines, salvias, and violas," her mother said as she put another chrysanthemum into a planter. "These chrysanthemums back here have the tiny purple flowers. Remember? We got them last year from your grandmother. They're her favorite flowers for the altar."

Yuki breathed in the smell of silver-green leaves and wet roots. At her grandmother's black Buddhist altar, the scent of chrysanthemums mingled with the white smoke from the incense and the steam from the freshly brewed tea. Yuki's grandmother grew several varieties of chrysanthemums, some with petals as thin as silk threads, others with dark red and yellow flowers, large as a heart. All of them were offered at the altar in their seasons.

"Maybe she can give us the big red ones this fall," Yuki said. "Those are my favorite."

"Are they?" Her mother stopped digging. "I always wondered if the dead people can really smell those flowers your grandmother offers them—and the tea and the rice, too. You know my older brother Susumu died in the War. I try to imagine his spirit coming back to that room, but I can't. Maybe he doesn't care about those flowers. He scarcely noticed anything in the garden when he was alive."

Yuki said nothing.

Her mother put her hand out, palm up, against the drizzle. "Maybe we get to be something like this rain when we die," she said. "We're there, but not really there. We'd be satisfied with just the smell of the chrysanthemums and the green tea. We wouldn't need much then."

Yuki felt a chill down her back, like the times her mother told her ghost stories. But that was for the hot summer nights when they couldn't sleep. Being scared was supposed to keep them cool, like taking a cold bath. "Mama, are you trying to scare me?" she asked. "It's only April and cold. I don't want to hear ghost stories yet."

Her mother resumed her digging. "I'm sorry," she said. "I didn't mean to scare you. Why don't you go back in the house? I'll be done here very soon."

"Are you sure? I can sit here and hold the umbrella. I packed everything already. I'm ready to clean up the rooms."

"It's not raining that much now. Why don't you go inside and finish cleaning?"

"All right." Yuki got up and went back into the house.

By the time she had swept the kitchen and the living room and was starting to clean her mother's room, the rain was coming down harder again. She heard her mother enter the house through the back door. Soon, she was standing in the hallway looking into the room. Yuki bent down to sweep the dust into the dustpan.

"I didn't have time to mark the boxes," Yuki said. "I guess you'll have to ask me where everything is. Don't worry. I'll remember."

Her mother took a step into the room. She put her hand on the wall and stood leaning slightly sideways as though she was very tired or dizzy. "Thanks a lot, Yuki," she said. "You've done a good job."

37

"It was nothing." Yuki shrugged.

Her mother hesitated, her hand still on the wall. Finally, she said, "I want to ask you something."

"What?" Yuki emptied the dustpan into the paper bag in the corner.

"Let's sit down."

"Here?"

"No. Let's go sit on the back steps. You can see the flowers I dug up."

They walked around the house and sat side by side on the narrow steps behind the kitchen. The boxes of plants were below them on the landing by the door. Her mother's black raincoat hung on the wall. From the window in the door, Yuki could see the rain, coming down harder now, blurring the line of ginkgo trees in the yard. The plants were green and wet from the rain: columbines with new leaves like rosebuds, violas and salvias and tiger lilies, a peony bush, three kinds of chrysanthemums.

"These look good," she said. "How about the irises?"

"They're already sending up spikes. We should leave them. They'll just die if we dig them out now."

"That's a shame." Yuki peered out the window. The irises were planted in a patch close to the house. Though she couldn't see them from this angle, she, too, had noticed the long spikes of buds shooting up among their fan-shaped leaves. In a few weeks, they would bloom—large flowers with dark purple outer petals, the pale inner petals, the splash of yellow at the center.

"Somebody will notice them," her mother said. "They're so pretty. I know they'll be cared for."

"All right." Yuki nodded.

Her mother leaned toward her and straightened out

Yuki's ponytail. "I want to ask you this now," she said. "What would you do if something happened to me? If I wasn't here anymore?" She put her arm around Yuki's shoulders.

"Why are you asking me?"

"Oh, I don't know. I was thinking of that day last winter when we packed your grandmother's things. Your father didn't cry at her funeral, remember? She was his mother."

It had been raining also on that day at her father's parents' house. Yuki hadn't been particularly sad herself. Though her father's parents lived just an hour's train ride away, she had seen them only once every few years. They didn't seem much like family to her.

"My father didn't cry because he didn't like her very much. He doesn't like anybody very much. Why should he cry?"

"But how about you? You'll forget me someday too. You'll go on without me."

Yuki turned sideways and pulled back slowly so that her mother had to let go of her shoulders. Yuki leaned back against the wall and looked her in the eyes.

"I won't forget you, ever," she said.

"Still, you would go on," her mother said. "Tell me the truth. You used to say I was the person you liked the most in the whole world and you'd never want to grow up because then I would be old and we wouldn't be together anymore. Do you still think that?"

Yuki sat perfectly still. Outside the window, the rain was hitting the irises and making a garbled noise like the radio after the stations had signed off. Yuki tried to imagine the large purple irises rising up on the long spikes like flames on candles, hundreds of them coming up from the wet ground. She thought of jumping over their purple fire. Her mother was waiting for her answer. Yuki turned back to her. "If something happened to you," she said, "I would still go on. I would be very sad. I would never forget you. Still, I would go on. It wouldn't be true to say otherwise."

Her mother slowly turned her head sideways and pressed her temple against the wall. Her eyes were squeezed shut. Yuki flung herself toward her, but her mother remained leaning away into the wall. Yuki took her hands. They were cold, fingers clenched tight. "Mama, I'm sorry," she said. "I didn't say that to hurt you. I wouldn't have said it if I thought it would make you upset. I'm so sorry."

Her mother didn't say anything for a long time. Finally, she turned back to Yuki and pulled her hands away.

"I'm sorry," Yuki said again.

Her mother laid her hands on Yuki's shoulders and pushed her back gently. She tilted her head a little and looked into Yuki's face. "Listen, Yuki," she said. "You were telling the truth. Don't apologize for that. I'm not really sad. You should always tell the truth." She sighed but nodded. "I'm glad you said you'd go on without me. You are a strong person. That's good." She leaned forward slowly and hugged her.

Yuki hugged her back hard. "I don't want you to talk about how you won't be here someday," she said, her voice muffled against her mother's hair.

Her mother didn't answer. Yuki pulled back to see her face. Her lips were drawn tight, as if she was trying not to cry.

"Mama, I'll help you all I can at the new house,"

Yuki said. "We'll have the best garden we've ever had. We'll start a new iris patch. We'll get Grandma to give us some white ones and yellow ones, too, even though I like the purple best." She stopped. Her voice was shaky. She took a deep breath.

"All right." Her mother stroked Yuki's hair. "All right. We'll try and have a good summer and fall. We'll try and be happy at the new house." She smiled with her lips closed.

"Mama," Yuki said, "you know I'll help you all I can. You know I'll do anything."

"Yes, I know," her mother said, patting her slowly on the back. "I know you will."

Outside, the rain kept making its garbled noises, sounding far away and nearby at once.

Yuki could no longer hear the TV from her father's room. She was done with her boxes. She went downstairs. Her father's room was open, but no one was there. Her stepmother's car was gone from where she parked it in front of the house. Yuki stepped outside and walked around to the backyard.

Her stepmother had done nothing to change the yard as yet. The irises Yuki and her mother had planted that fall were sending up their long spikes just like those from the old house. Toward the back, columbines had grown into large bushes and spread. In a month, they would blossom—red, yellow, purple, and pink flowers growing from the same stem, with long plumes like festival lanterns. Yuki went to the middle of the yard and stood by the patch of chrysanthemums and violas. Overhead, some sparrows were chirping in the maples.

Her mother was right about the flowers. They were

hardy. They were getting ready to blossom another year. Her mother had thought that Yuki, too, would go on without her. Yuki had said so, two years ago, as they looked at these same chrysanthemums and violas. She should never have believed me, Yuki thought. Three sparrows fluttered down from the maples and chased each other to the neighbor's yard. They came back and landed near the irises. Yuki walked over to the patch and sat down beside the flowers. Soon, the purple and yellow flowers would climb up the long spikes and open, one by one. Irises flowered sparingly, unlike the roses and peonies that bloomed all at once and shed. When the irises faded, they shriveled into themselves like punctured balloons and dried up; not a petal fell to the ground. Yuki stood up and turned away from the garden.

Mama, she thought as she walked toward the house. Maybe I was wrong when I said I could go on alone. But you wouldn't let me take it back. I wanted to take it back.

5
Pink Trumpets
(June 1971)

The man in the white uniform was drawing fresh chalk lines on the track with something that looked like a small lawn mower. Limbering up on the grass slightly apart from the other girls, Yuki watched the orderly parallel lines he was leaving behind on the caked dirt. There was still another hour to wait before the first event, perhaps two hours or more before the 1,000 meters Yuki was going to run. Some of the parents were already arriving to find seats on the bleachers: this was the last girls' track meet before the summer vacation—city finals for the junior high school of Kobe.

Yuki shaded her eyes with her hand and looked toward the bleachers, at the women in their white summer blouses, dark skirts, and pale pink, turquoise, or mint-green parasols. The early crowd was mostly mothers, although the meet had been scheduled on a Sunday morning so fathers could attend. Your mother would have been proud, Yuki told herself. She had gotten into the habit of saying this to herself in the two years since her mother's death. It was what every adult except her father and his new wife had said when she did anything deserving of praise—winning in track meets, being elected president of her eighth-grade class, getting the highest marks every year. It was as though, as far as they, the other adults, were concerned, *Your mother would have been proud* was a great compliment, the highest form of praise. As for Yuki's father and his wife, they never mentioned her mother. They said very little of anything to her. There were days when hardly any words passed between Yuki and either of them.

She stretched out her legs in front of her and bent her upper body into them. Her face pressed against her knees, she held the stretch and thought about the picture her mother had taken on School Sports Day when Yuki was in third grade. It showed her passing the girl ahead of her and winning the 50-meter dash. Her mother had pressed the shutter at precisely the right moment. Yuki's left shoulder and right leg had just gotten in front of the other girl, although the rest of their bodies were still in line. In the far corner of the picture, the finish-line tape blurred white. Yuki was wearing a huge white silk ribbon tied like a butterfly around her long hair, which was pulled back and then braided. Her mother had made her wear the ribbon "so I can recognize you right away even from a distance," she had said. Her mother was always like that—tying big ribbons round Yuki's hair, knitting her sweaters in bright red or purple or turquoise, colors that made her stand out.

For another minute, Yuki remained bent double, pressing her face harder into her knees. Since her mother's death, she had her hair cut so short that from the back, people often thought she was a boy. She could sometimes recognize the look of surprise when they heard her voice and realized that she was a girl.

When she looked up from her stretch, a group of girls in red-and-black uniforms were just passing by. They were from the only private, all-girls school left in the competition. Yuki hurriedly glanced in front of her and then behind her and found the tall ninth-grade girl who ran hurdles. She was bringing up the rear with the short-haired, almost plump girl who seemed to be her close friend. The hurdler had long hair—Yuki imagined it would come down to her waist when she had it loose—which she wore in a thick ponytail, baring her long white neck. Her skin was fair even after a season of track practice in the sun. As she passed by Yuki, she smiled, her lips curving upward just a little, not showing her teeth at all. Yuki smiled back and then looked down at her own knees. She thought that she heard the other girl, the plump one, suppress a giggle. Her face felt hot. Of course they must have known she was staring; it was obvious. But then she really couldn't help it.

If she would only talk to me, Yuki thought. She must not mind my staring; otherwise she wouldn't smile.

The first time they had met, Yuki had just finished running the 1,000-meter event at the meet between their two schools. She came in first, beating a girl from the other school in the last ten meters. Then she went to get a drink of water and almost bumped into the tall girl. Yuki couldn't remember now exactly what she had noticed about her first—her beautiful hair, her face, which looked cool even in the sun, her long neck, or perhaps just how tall she really was. But about ten minutes after almost bumping into her, Yuki saw her run the hurdles—her legs just sailing, a pair of graceful arcs. When she came in first, a good five meters ahead of the second runner, who was from Yuki's school, Yuki nearly jumped up and cheered. She caught herself with her hands in front of her, about to start clapping. The girls from Yuki's school were silent because their teammates hadn't won. Sitting among them, Yuki felt almost sorry for them. How can they not notice her? she wondered. Since then, there had been three invitational meets and the one semifinals meet in which Yuki had watched the tall, graceful hurdler.

If she would only talk to me, Yuki thought again. Then I would be happy for the rest of today, and perhaps even longer.

By the time her turn came to run, it was past noon. The sun was hot, the air humid. The heat vapors rising from the grass reminded her of the long summer days she had spent with her mother, working in the garden, picnicking, hiking, swimming. The days back then had seemed endless.

She was assigned the outside lane, which she preferred. It was much better than being inside and having eight or nine runners bearing down on you in the dash to the first straightaway. While she waited for the signal, Yuki closed her eyes momentarily and reminded herself of the way the tall girl had just won her race. She had come in first again, five or six strides in front. The results were not official yet, but it was said that she had broken the meet record. I must win too, Yuki thought.

When the gun went off, she was still thinking of the tall girl and also of the summer days she had spent with her mother. Then she was running and the air was a blue blur.

Coming to the first straightaway, she was in third place behind the two girls in red and black, runners from the same school as the tall girl. Yuki decided to stay behind them. A few runners always pushed the pace in the first two laps and dropped back in the third or fourth lap. The ones she had to watch out for were those who were still behind her now. She swung her arms, nice and easy, reminding herself to relax her shoulders, her sides.

At the beginning of the second lap, Yuki felt her heartbeat rock her body even though her breathing felt relaxed. It was just her heart. As always, she had this flashing thought: I wonder if anybody ever passes out from nervousness. Almost the same moment that she repeated the thought to herself, the lightheadedness was gone and her heart no longer beat so hard. This, too, was how it always was. About halfway through the second lap, she always had this brief moment of panic, which went away as soon as she noticed it.

Going into the third lap, she thought, almost halfway through. This was usually the lap to relax a little, to save up for the last two laps, in which she would gradually surge so that she was running as fast as she possibly could in the latter half of the fifth lap. At least that was how she had always won. It seemed like a good strategy. Still, she had often won by only a very small margin, trying to shake off the other runners in the last twenty or thirty meters, hearing them breathing behind her till the last moment.

The two runners ahead of her were beginning to falter. Directly behind her, two or three others were running in step. She could hear their breathing, rather hard and loud already. She wondered if hers sounded like that to them. To herself, it sounded quite easy, much more relaxed than theirs. The next moment, before she even knew it herself, she was speeding up. She quickly passed the two girls ahead of her, then realized that she had committed herself, perhaps too soon. There was a good three quarters of the third lap still left to go, then the fourth, and then the fifth. She would have to keep up the pace now and not let the others pass her back.

Several seconds later, coming to the end of the third lap, Yuki began to run as fast as she could. She kept listening to her own breathing, rhythmically repeating to herself, I'll make it, I'll make it, stifling about every ten steps the terrible recurring voice that said, You made a mistake, you'll never finish.

By the time she was beginning the last lap, her shoulders hurt—sharp pains like knife points. She was breathing hard, very hard by now. Only another lap, she told herself, I can hurt for another lap. She no longer heard anyone behind her. She couldn't tell if they were too far back or if the loudness of her own breathing and heartbeat had deafened her.

As she sprinted down the last straightaway to the finish, Yuki could almost see the black point of pain. She kept it in front of her, where she could squint at it and still not lose sight of the track, of the orderly parallel lines the man had drawn earlier, only by now not so orderly—fading in places even, a little crooked. To keep going when there's no air, she thought. Is this how it was, Mama? Was it painful? More painful than this, far more painful. I can remember the smell of gas and you on the floor, not breathing, and Father saying later that you did not suffer, it did not hurt, did not hurt.

As she crossed the finish line, the black blur of her thought was replaced by the white blur of the uniforms of the other girls on her team. They were all surrounding her—she was leaning on somebody's arm—and they were saying how she had won by a big margin, how she must have broken the record, how the others were way behind her. As her breaths slowed down and the pain spread through her body and then faded, Yuki stood alone on the grass and thought: I didn't even look back; I didn't know where the others were.

All the events were over by one thirty. There was a late lunch break while the results were being computed. The girls on Yuki's team dispersed to find their families. Yuki ran toward the drinking fountain before anybody could ask her what she was going to do for lunch, would she care to join their family? Everyone knew that Yuki's mother was dead, that nobody from her family ever came to the meets.

Yuki had not even brought lunch. In the morning, when she came down to the kitchen for a glass of orange juice, her stepmother had looked at her without a word. "I'm going to the track meet," Yuki told her. "I'll be back in the afternoon, not too late." Her stepmother still said nothing. Yuki added hastily, "And I won't need lunch. I can't run and eat. It'll just make me sick." After that, she drank up the orange juice and ran out of the kitchen. Her stepmother had said nothing at all. The last time her stepmother had really talked to her was more than a year ago. "Please don't keep asking me so many questions about what you can do to help me," she had said. They were in the midst of dinner and her stepmother had suddenly put down her chopsticks and turned to her. "If you have to ask, then there's no point in it. What's the use of having you help me clean if you can't even tell when things are clean or dirty, if you have to ask? If you can't do it without being told, then just try not to get in my way. And don't talk so much all the time. I've put up with it so far because I heard that you were a very smart child and maybe smart children talk more than the not-so-smart ones. But I'm sick of it. I've really had enough." Her stepmother then collected her dishes, put them in the sink, and left the table. Yuki had sat with her father, who went on eating in silence as though nothing had happened. Since then, Yuki and her stepmother never said much to each other.

Yuki ran toward the fountain. By now, her teammates would be climbing up the bleachers toward their mothers, who would be waving to them and saying, "Here you are. Look what I brought you for lunch. Hurry and sit down." Yuki counted her steps, one, two, one, two, and repeated to herself, It's nothing, I'm all right, it's nothing.

She stopped in front of the fountain and took a deep breath. She realized that she was looking down at the long ponytail of the tall hurdler. She was bending over the fountain to drink water, and Yuki was staring at the back of her white neck. The next moment, the girl raised her head, looked back, and smiled.

"Always running into each other at drinking fountains, aren't we?" the girl said.

In confusion, Yuki plunged her face into the stream of water. It was surprisingly cold. She drank fast, almost suffocating, and then looked up. The girl was still standing, waiting for her.

"I'm Yuki," Yuki said. She swallowed hard. "Yuki Okuda. I ran in the 1,000 meters." She didn't know what else to say.

"I know," the girl said. "I saw you come in first."

50

"I saw you come in first too," Yuki said. "Way ahead of the others."

"I'm Sachiko Murai. Did you know my name?"

"No. But I've watched you." Yuki felt her face turning red.

"I knew your name," Sachiko Murai said. "I've heard a lot about you. I know some people who go to your school. They said that you were one of the best runners at their school even though you were only in eighth grade and this is your first year in track. Not only that, you're very bright and you're president of your class. You beat the boy who ran against you because your speeches were so good. That's very rare, isn't it, for a girl to win the election and become president of her class at a coed school?" Sachiko paused.

Yuki could think of nothing to say. She couldn't even just say "Yes," because it would sound like bragging.

"Anyway," Sachiko continued, "my friends said that they admired you a lot because you've done so well in everything even though . . ." Sachiko fell silent. "But I shouldn't say such a thing."

"Even though what?"

"I really shouldn't say."

"I want you to tell me."

"All right, even though your mother's passed away and your father and stepmother never come to see you run or make speeches or anything. There, I've said it."

Yuki considered this for a moment. Then she said, with a boldness that surprised even herself, "Are you sorry for me?"

Sachiko seemed to hesitate. "Do you want me to be?"

"No," Yuki said firmly. "Never."

"All right, then I won't be."

They walked together for a few minutes in silence, passing some families who were sitting on the grass with their picnic lunches. Young children were running around and laughing.

"So what are you going to do this summer vacation?" Sachiko was asking her.

"I don't know," Yuki said. She hadn't thought of it till now—the long days without school, her stepmother silent in the kitchen, her father coming home and just nodding toward Yuki, not saying a word. Every day would be like the Sundays before she joined the track team, when she stayed home all day, cooped up in her room. She tried to find something to say. If I don't, she thought, Sachiko will decide her friends were wrong after all and I'm stupid. But nothing came to her mind.

"I don't live very far from you," Sachiko said, "even though I go to the private school because both my sisters went there. That's how I know the people who go to your school. I went to grade school with them. Maybe we can run together once in a while to stay in shape. Do you want to? You're going out for cross-country in the fall, right? Maybe we can meet in Uzumoridai Park. You live near there, don't you? I think I saw you running there once."

"Yes," Yuki said. She could only speak very softly. She wondered if Sachiko would mistake it to mean that she wasn't enthusiastic about running with her. "I would like so much to run with you," Yuki added, trying to control her voice. "I do live near that park, and I'm going out for cross-country in the fall."

"Good," Sachiko said. "Come with me then. I'm supposed to meet my mother for lunch where the azaleas are, near the parking lot. She probably has a pen in her purse, so we can exchange phone numbers."

The woman sitting by the azaleas was smoking a long cigarette with a gold circle drawn where her fingers held it. Yuki would have guessed her to be Sachiko's mother even if she had seen them separately. She was tall like Sachiko and fair. Unlike other mothers, who wore white blouses and dark skirts shaped like tea cozies, Sachiko's mother was wearing a slim green dress and carrying a green purse made of cloth. She crushed out the cigarette against the bottom of the stone bench and dropped it on the ground.

"Mother, this is Yuki Okuda. She won the 1,000 meters and broke the record, just like I did at the hurdles."

"Hello." Mrs. Murai smiled. "I saw you. You looked so much smaller than the other girls. Someone sitting near me said that you were one of the few eighth graders who made it to the finals." Mrs. Murai then turned away from Yuki toward her daughter. She reached out her hand and smoothed Sachiko's hair with her long fingers. "Your hair's all tangled up."

"Is it?" Sachiko said absentmindedly. She shook her head impatiently under her mother's fingers.

"You should have let me put it up. Then it wouldn't have gotten so tangled. Turn around."

"It's not so bad as it is," Sachiko said, all the same turning around for her mother.

Mrs. Murai took a brush out of her purse, pulled off the rubber band that was holding Sachiko's ponytail, and began to brush her hair.

"Mother, you're hurting my scalp. Don't pull so hard."

"Really, you ought to take better care of your hair."

"But I don't even want long hair. For all I care, I could cut it short like Yuki's. Look at her hair, Mother. Isn't it nice and simple? I'm sure it's easier to take care of than mine. I'd like that."

Mrs. Murai glanced back at Yuki. She seemed doubtful.

"I won't hear about you cutting your hair," she said to her daughter.

Sachiko looked toward Yuki and rolled her eyes, as if to say, You know how they are.

But I don't, anymore, Yuki thought.

Finally, Mrs. Murai put the brush back in her purse and let go of Sachiko. "Leave your hair like that. You don't have to tie it up again now, do you? I left our lunch in the car, so we'll have to go get it." She turned to Yuki questioningly.

Sachiko looked from her mother to Yuki and then back.

Her hair, Yuki noticed, was really down to her waist. It made her look slightly older than her age. Yuki noted exactly how much she looked like her mother—the long oval face, perfectly arched eyebrows.

"We wanted to see if you had a pen," Yuki said to Mrs. Murai.

"Yuki and I are going to run together during summer vacation," Sachiko explained. "We wanted to exchange phone numbers. You must have a pen in your purse, Mother."

"Oh, I see. How nice." Mrs. Murai began to rummage through her purse. "But I can't find a pen," she said after a while. "It's very strange. I usually do carry one around." She continued to look. "I'm so sorry to keep you waiting like this. Your family must be wondering where you've gone. They must be so proud of you."

"Mother," Sachiko said. Her voice sounded alarmed, or possibly just embarrassed. Yuki could not tell which.

"What is it?"

"Oh, it's nothing," Yuki said. "I'd better be going." She said to Sachiko, "If you give me your phone number, I'll memorize it."

"Are you sure?" Sachiko said. "But of course, you must have a good memory."

"I'll try, anyhow."

"Al right. It's 25-3794—25-3794. Can you remember that?"

"I'll remember."

"It was very nice to meet you," Mrs. Murai said, already turning away.

Sachiko shrugged, smiled, and waved. She began to walk beside her mother.

Yuki watched the two of them walking close together until she could no longer see them. Then she looked toward the stone bench where Mrs. Murai had been sitting. All around the bench, azalea bushes were in full bloom, some of them pale pink, the others bright, almost purplish pink. A long time ago, Yuki remembered, her mother had shown her how to pick an azalea blossom and pull off the calyx so that all the stamens came out and what was left of the flower was like a little trumpet. Then she would gently blow out the pollen that had scattered, and taste the inside of the flower with the tip of her tongue. Where the petals came together and narrowed like the mouth of the trumpet, there were spots of intense sweetness—so intense that her tongue tingled. Sometimes, the pale flowers were spotted bright red inside. These were the sweetest of them all.

Suddenly faint, Yuki sat down on the stone bench. Still repeating the number Sachiko had given her, rapidly, fervently, she remained for a long time gazing at the azaleas. She wished she could eat the flowers, thousands of pink trumpets, and suffocate with their sweetness.

6

Sundays
(September 1971)

The first week of September had been unusually cool. On Sunday morning, Yuki put on a long-sleeved T-shirt over her shorts to go running. Her father and stepmother were having their breakfast in the kitchen. As she went down the stairs, Yuki could smell the tea and the salted fish her stepmother was cooking. She went out the front door and started running toward the park, where she was meeting Sachiko.

Along the road, the chestnut trees were heavy with green spiked balls. In a month, the balls would burst, and the pavement would be covered with shiny black nuts that cracked underfoot. Soon after that, Yuki would be running in the cross-country meets every Sunday. The second term of school had started the week before. At the first cross-country practice on Wednesday, the coach had said everyone should take weekends off from running until the meets started. "Resting is as important as running," he said. "You'll be training every weekday after school. That's enough running." "But I run with a friend on Sundays," Yuki said. "We've been doing it all summer." "You should stop after this coming Sunday," he said. "I don't want you pushing yourself too hard and getting hurt or sick."

It doesn't matter, Yuki thought as she approached the white gate of the park. Sachiko would have started practicing at her school. Most likely, her coach would want her to rest on Sundays as well. Soon, they would be running against each other for the first time: they had been in different events in track, and last year, Yuki wasn't on the cross-country team while Sachiko was winning and setting records. Maybe I won't be very good anyway, Yuki thought as she entered the park and headed for the blue bench next to the drinking fountain.

It was nine o'clock, the time they had agreed to meet, but Sachiko was always a few minutes late. Yuki stopped by the bench and waited, jumping up and down to stay warm. She tried to think of a way to tell Sachiko that they should continue meeting every week—but what could they do together besides running? Yuki wasn't sure. "To get together and talk" sounded silly or forward or both. Girls in high school or college sat in coffee shops for hours talking, but she and Sachiko were only in eighth and ninth grades. "To go to a movie" wasn't quite right either. Yuki sometimes went to movies with friends, but never with just one of them. Nobody saw movies with just one other person, except older girls on dates. It was hopeless. Even if she could think of something they might do together, she wouldn't know how to bring it up in the half hour they would be running. She and Sachiko had run together once a week all summer and never done anything else except for drinking orange juice afterward at Sachiko's house— and that was only the first few times they met, back in late June.

Yuki spotted Sachiko coming up the path in red tights and a white T-shirt, her hair done up into a bun.

Sachiko waved; her palm flashed red in a fingerless glove. Yuki ran to meet her.

"Hope you weren't waiting long," Sachiko said, smiling.

"No, not at all."

They left the park, which was at the bottom of a long hill. Above, houses were built along the flat east-west streets, with the north-south streets intersecting at a sharp incline. Yuki and Sachiko always took the same four-mile route. From the park, they ran five blocks west, went uphill a block, turned east and ran five blocks, then uphill another block to head west. They continued to weave back and forth on the flat streets, always going uphill at the end, until they were at the top of the ridge overlooking the city. The route had been Sachiko's idea. "It's good to run hills," she said. "You can use different muscles that way."

"So how was your first week of school?" Sachiko asked when they came to the end of the first block.

"All right," Yuki answered. "I went to cross-country practice after school. We started on Wednesday." She paused, wondering if she should mention not running on weekends. She glanced sideways at Sachiko's face. A wisp of hair, gotten loose from her bun, fluttered up and down next to her cheek. No, she thought. Too soon. "How was your week?" she asked.

"Good," Sachiko said, "except for something really strange that happened to me on the train."

"What's that?"

"Well, you know how you keep seeing the same people if you take the same train to school every day?"

"Yes," Yuki said, though she had never taken a train to school. She walked to the public school near her house, while Sachiko rode the commuter train to her private school in the suburbs.

"On the train, there was a boy who kept staring at me. He was tall and thin, with long hair almost down to his shoulders. Every day from Monday to Thursday, he ended up standing next to me. He got on one stop after mine, so he might have been looking for me."

They were at the end of their first five blocks. They fell silent as they picked up the pace and sprinted up-hill.

"Anyway," Sachiko continued once they had turned east and slowed down, "on Friday, he came on the train again. He must go to the boys' high school in eastern Kobe. He gets off two stops before me. On the first four days, he nodded and smiled at me before he got off."

"He smiled? But you didn't know him?" Yuki asked. "Maybe it's someone you went to grade school with and forgot."

"No," Sachiko said. "You're funny."

Yuki looked away. What she said had been stupid. Still, if she met somebody from fifth grade, she might never recognize him. Grade school seemed like a long time ago, when she lived in another part of town with her mother.

"It's no one I knew before," Sachiko said. "I'm sure because I know his name now."

"Oh. How did that come about?"

"I was trying to tell you before you interrupted me."

"I'm sorry."

"On Friday, when the door opened at his stop, he smiled and stuck his hand out, like he was going to shake my hand. Next thing I knew, he'd slipped something into my hand, the door was closing, and he was running out. He barely made it. He waved at me from the platform. The train started moving. What he gave me turned out to be a corner torn from a notebook with his name and phone number written on it. Can you imagine that? He expected me to call him." Sachiko smiled and shook her head.

"He said that on the paper?"

"No, no. The paper had only his name and phone number. But why would he be writing them down if he didn't expect me to call?"

They were coming to the corner. In someone's yard to their right, yellow marigolds and pink snapdragons looked faded since the cool weather. The petals had begun to curl at the edges. Soon, the frost would break them into a pile of broken stems. Sprinting uphill, Yuki concentrated on pumping her arms as the incline shortened her stride. Sachiko finished first and ran in place. Yuki caught up and they slowed down.

"So you're going to call him?" Yuki asked.

Sachiko almost stopped as she turned sideways to face Yuki. Then she shook her head and continued running, staring straight ahead. "I can't believe you would think that about me," she said.

"Think what?"

"Come on, Yuki. I'm not going to call a boy I don't know, just because that's what he wants. Nobody does that."

"But I thought—" Yuki stopped. "Never mind," she said. Her face felt hot.

"You thought what?" Sachiko was frowning.

"I don't know what I was saying."

"Tell me what you were going to say. It's rude to

start saying something and stop. Now I'll be wondering what you were going to say."

"Okay." Yuki shrugged. "I was going to say that you sounded like you might want to call him."

Sachiko said nothing for two blocks. Yuki looked down at the blacktop. There were no sidewalks this far up the hill. In July and August, bubbles had burst on the surface of the road and tar stuck to the soles of their shoes. Now, there were small scars of darker black where the road had melted. Yuki wished she had said something else.

"So how did I sound like I wanted to call him?" Sachiko asked her finally.

"I don't know. You sounded—well, you sounded like you weren't upset about his staring at you, for one thing." Her own voice sounded whiny and stupid, but it was too late not to go on with the truth.

"How is that? What did I say that made you think that?"

"I don't know. I think maybe I was mistaken about the whole thing. Can we stop talking about this?"

"No. You must have had some reason."

"Okay." Yuki sighed. "Maybe you would have taken a different train if you had really minded."

"I would be late for school if I took a later train."

"You could have taken an earlier one."

"Let me tell you something." Sachiko's voice was quiet and icy. "I'm not going to get up half an hour earlier and catch a different train because some boy has a crush on me and stares at me. That's his problem. I won't go out of my way because of that."

Yuki didn't answer. The more she said, the worse it was.

"What would you do," Sachiko asked, "if some boy stared at you like that?" She didn't give Yuki time to answer. She took off in a sprint for the rest of the block and up the hill.

Breathing hard to keep up, Yuki tried to think of the right answer but couldn't. At her school, boys and girls weren't together much outside classes. At lunch, boys sat with boys, girls with girls. It was the same in the library or at assembly. Even in sports after school, boys' teams and girls' teams didn't practice together. Some afternoons when she ran along the fence that separated the track from the baseball field, Yuki heard the players calling to each other. Their voices sounded so ugly, choked up and croaking. Most of the boys in the field were tall and bony. They were much taller than she was. Yuki couldn't believe that only a few years ago she used to have fistfights with boys in grade school and win. If she went up to the baseball players and tried to punch them, they would only laugh at her. They wouldn't even take offense.

She caught up with Sachiko on the next flat street and said, "If a boy stared at me, I would think I had put on the wrong skirt with my blouse so they didn't match and the boy was laughing at me. Or else there's a smudge on my face or my hair might be sticking out a funny way."

Sachiko burst out laughing. "Oh, Yuki," she said. "You're so innocent."

"I'm not being funny," Yuki insisted. "Those would be the only reasons a boy would stare at me. No one has ever had a crush on me."

"I'm sure you're wrong." Sachiko smiled.

They ran on in silence. Yuki remembered one of the

few times when she and her mother had been really angry at each other, back when she was in sixth grade. They were in the fabric section of a department store. Her mother wanted to get a pattern for Yuki's new dress. She held up one that had a lace collar and a bow that tied in the back. She said she would make it in pink. Yuki said, "I don't want a pink dress. I hate the lace on the collar. And the bow makes it look like an apron." In the end, they walked away without choosing a pattern. Shizuko needed some new pots and pans from the kitchen section. When a clerk came to help them, Yuki and her mother both smiled at her and chatted but said nothing to each other. After her mother bought the pots and pans, they walked on in silence. Halfway down the stairs that led to the exit, Yuki said, "Mama, I just want you to know something. I'm not clammed up because I'm sulking on purpose. I'm not acting childish. I'm truly too angry to speak." Her mother stopped and grabbed hold of the handrail because she was suddenly laughing. "Yuki," she said between gasps of laughter. "You are simply too much." Yuki started laughing then because come to think of it, what she said was ridiculous. That had been the end of their argument.

But this was different. Though Yuki was relieved that Sachiko was not angry anymore, she didn't think what she had said was funny. It was just the truth.

Soon, they were at the top of the hill. They slowed down as they ran along the ridge. The city stretched below—a thin strip of green, white, and brown between the mountains and the sea. Yuki followed the curve of the coast to the area she had lived in till fifth grade. Her old house was five blocks from the sea. From the kitchen window, she used to see one of the pine trees planted by the breakwater. It looked like a fox wearing a long dress. "The fox in a wedding dress," she and her mother had called it. From the ridge, she could pick out the green blur where the pines were.

"Ready for the last leg?" Sachiko asked.

Yuki nodded.

They turned south and went downhill. As usual, Sachiko picked up the pace in the last four blocks, and Yuki struggled to keep up. She would have a better chance, she knew, if they sped up sooner or much later. In track, she was good at a short all-out kick at the end or else a long steady surge, not the medium kick Sachiko chose. As usual, she finished several steps behind her friend inside the park, both of them bent over and panting with their hands on their knees. Gradually, they straightened up and walked to the drinking fountain. Though it was cool, they were still thirsty. They drank and then sat on the grass to stretch.

"It was a lot of fun running with you this summer," Sachiko said as, side by side, they bent their knees into the hurdler's stretch.

"Maybe we could continue somehow," Yuki said.

Sachiko said nothing. She switched her legs and bent the other way.

"My coach says we should take weekends off, but I don't know. What does yours say?"

Sachiko pulled her knees to her chest and sat with her chin on her kneecaps. "I'm not going out for cross-country after all."

"What?" Yuki sat up and crossed her ankles.

Sachiko shrugged. "I'm going to be in the school play in November. I have the leading part. We tried out the last week of vacation and just found out the results on Thursday."

Yuki said nothing. The breeze made her shiver.

"We rehearse almost every day after school, so I can't make the practice."

"Well," Yuki said, "maybe you can still be on the team anyway, by practicing on your own. You're so good. I bet your coach wouldn't mind."

"She already talked to me. She said she could meet me an hour before school and watch me run."

"So?"

"I said I couldn't."

"Why not?"

"My mother doesn't want me to be in the play and on the team both. She's afraid I'd be tired and sick, or I wouldn't have time for homework and my grades would drop." Sachiko picked at the grass.

Yuki pulled her long sleeves over her hands. Her fingers were freezing. The back of her T-shirt was soaked from her sweat.

"You're cold," Sachiko noticed. "Here. Let's get going." She stood up.

They walked across the grass toward the park entrance.

"I don't mind about missing cross-country," Sachiko said. "I did well last year. I don't want to be under a lot of pressure this year to break my own records, or watch someone else break them." She paused and smiled. "You, for instance. When I read about your new records in the paper, I'll be happy because I won't be running anymore myself. I'm very competitive. I can't stand losing."

"But you'll always beat me."

66

They stopped at the gate. Sachiko lived five blocks southwest and Yuki four blocks east.

"All summer, you finished first," Yuki said. "I could hardly keep up."

"I finished first because you let me."

"That's not true. I would never lose on purpose."

"But you could have sped up sooner without waiting for me to choose the right time for myself. You could have pushed the pace before I was ready." Sachiko put her hand on the white fence that stretched along the outside of the park. "Isn't that true?"

"I don't know."

"Believe me, you're good enough to beat me, especially once your coach starts training you."

But I don't want to beat you, Yuki thought but didn't say.

"Well," Sachiko said. "Thank you for running with me all summer."

"Maybe I can talk to my coach," Yuki said. "I can ask for one day off practice so I can run with you on Sundays, at least until the meets start up. You'll keep running on your own to stay in shape for indoor track in January, right? The play will be over long before that."

"It's very kind of you to think of me. Don't change your schedule to suit me, though."

"I wouldn't mind. Even if the coach doesn't let me off, I can run on Sundays anyway. He doesn't have to know about it."

Sachiko took her hand off the fence and pushed the stray hair out of her face. "The thing is," she said, "I'll be busy on Sundays. My mother wants me to start taking flower arrangement lessons. I'll be in high school

67

come April. She thinks it's time for me to stop being such a tomboy and learn something feminine."

"You'll still go out for track, won't you?"

"I'm not sure. We'll have to see."

Sachiko shrugged, the corners of her lips turned down slightly. Yuki kicked at the grass with her toes. In flower arrangement, Sachiko would sit Zen-style on the floor with her legs folded under, feet tucked in. Yuki imagined her long fingers clenched around small, sharp scissors as she cut through the thick stems of lilies, irises, birds-of-paradise. She would wind thin wires tight around the flowers and stick them into small clusters of needles to keep them standing straight. The flowers must hurt, Yuki used to think every time she saw such traditional arrangements at restaurants or teahouses. Her mother had put garden flowers in big white urns and let them spill over every whichway just like they did outside. In flower arrangement, nothing looked the way it did in the garden.

"I hope to read about your running in the newspapers," Sachiko said. "Good luck, and thanks." She held out her right hand.

Yuki reached out. Sachiko's hand was warm even through the glove, her fingers smooth in contrast to the grainy texture of the cloth. Yuki's hand was freezing. They shook and let go.

"You'd better get home before you catch a cold," Sachiko said. "See you around," she said as she walked away.

"Yes, see you around," Yuki said more loudly than she had intended. Sachiko was only a few steps away. She didn't look back.

Yuki stood and watched Sachiko as she rounded the

corner and disappeared. She thought of the boy on the train. She wondered what his handwriting had looked like—perhaps it was small and cramped like her own; the more nervous he was, the more cramped. Yuki imagined him double checking his phone number to make sure it was right. Even his own number, which he must have known by heart, could have sounded strange to him when he thought of Sachiko's long hair or the way she smiled with her lips closed. As he slipped the paper into her palm, his heart must have beaten hard. He must have run out of the train in a panic as the doors came sliding shut, almost catching him in the middle.

Yuki walked down the street and stopped under the chestnut trees. She was shivering, but she didn't want to go home. She leaned back against the stone wall of someone's house.

"See you around," Sachiko had said, but she didn't really mean it. They would never meet again, Yuki thought, maybe not even by accident. Though their houses were close enough, they had never met until the track season in the spring.

Yuki looked up at the trees. She could remember, back in late May, when they were covered with white flowers that looked like long torches. Chestnuts flowered after the cherries and plums of April, before the wisteria and oranges of June. Spring and summer had been a long progression of trees flowering and shedding in turn. The last time Yuki had been invited to Sachiko's house after the run, the pomegranate tree in their front yard had been in flower. Its petals were glossy red and crinkled, almost as though they were made of paper. The flowers smelled like chewing gum or sticky candy. By now, the fruit would be ripe.

On that last visit, Sachiko's mother had sat in the kitchen with them while they drank their orange juice. Flicking the ashes from her cigarette on the side of her glass ashtray, Mrs. Murai asked Yuki what her family did for a living.

"My father works in an office downtown," she answered. "He's an engineer at the steel company. My mother's passed away. My father's remarried. She used to be his secretary, but she stays home now that they're married."

Mrs. Murai frowned. She crushed out her cigarette. "Well," she said, "you're so young to have lost your mother. That must be very hard. Was she ill for a long time?"

Sachiko had put down her glass and was looking at Yuki, waiting for an answer. Sachiko and her mother were sitting side by side across the table from Yuki. "No, my mother wasn't ill," Yuki said. "It was an accident."

"How terrible," Mrs. Murai said. "In a car?"

"No," Yuki said, feeling the blood rush to her face. "At home."

The room was quiet. Sachiko finished her juice and stood up to put the empty glass in the sink. She came back and sat down next to her mother. Yuki looked down at the table. The half glass she had drunk tasted sour in the back of her throat. She got up without finishing.

"I'd better go," she said, already heading for the door. Sachiko and her mother didn't get up from the table and say, "No, no, you must stay" the way people did when a guest was about to leave. They sat in silence. Yuki ran out of the house into the chewing-gum smell of the pomegranates. She was never asked back. Her father had told her to say that her mother had died of cancer, if anyone ever asked. There wasn't much else a person of her age could have died of. It was foolish to admit the truth and cause suspicions, her father had warned. People would say that she came from a mentally unstable family.

The stone wall was cold. Yuki began walking the rest of the way home. She continued to think of that day back in June. At least in her mind, she could go back and correct her mistake, making everything come out right.

The way she imagined it, the way it should have been, she would calmly finish her juice, put down the glass, and tell the truth.

"My mother died because she was unhappy," she would say. "It was no accident. She meant to die." And while Sachiko and her mother sat speechless with shock, Yuki would stand up and add, "I want to work hard and be happy for her because that's what she wanted. I promised her I'd go on. I want to live and be a good person."

Then slowly, Sachiko and her mother would stand up, come to her side of the table, and embrace her between them.

"Your mother would be so proud of you," they would say. "We're proud of you too. You are a strong person."

Yuki would have been asked to stay for breakfast, stay the whole day to watch a movie or play games or go shopping with them downtown. She would be there right now. Sundays before cross-country meets would have been days to spend with them. She'd have gone to

71

watch Sachiko at her flower arrangement lessons and play rehearsals.

Yuki stood in front of her house. Her stepmother's car was parked in front, lipstick red, a small dent in the front where she had hit a mailbox when her high heel got stuck in the gas pedal. That was two weeks ago. Her stepmother came home shaking, Yuki's father holding her hand, and spent the afternoon in bed. Later, she complained about how Yuki's footsteps upstairs had added to her headache and nausea. "You won't even let me rest," she said. "What do you do up there in your room anyway? What's all that pacing about?" "Nothing," Yuki said. "I read or draw pictures. Or I write letters and do my homework. That's all. Nothing much." Her stepmother screwed up her face as though everything Yuki said was somehow offensive. It didn't matter if Yuki was telling the truth. Her stepmother always acted like she was lying.

Yuki walked through the narrow space her stepmother had left between the car and the entrance. She opened the door, stepped into the dark foyer, and quickly glanced down the hallway. There was no one. Her father's room was shut, with the sound of TV coming from under the door. Yuki took off her shoes and climbed up the stairs holding her breath, trying not to make any noise. She entered her room and closed the door. She changed her shirt, put on long pants, and sat down at her desk, careful not to scrape the chair legs across the floor. Outside the window, the sky to the north was full of small clouds that looked like fish scales. The sky's changing, her mother would have said: it's fall. Yuki opened her sketchbook to draw the sky. She sighed. After today, there would be five Sundays before the cross-country meets started.

7
Yellow Mittens and Early Violets
(March 1972)

Masa stepped into the kitchen in her gray kimono and turned on the light. Her granddaughter Yuki was sitting at the table, putting on and pulling off her yellow mittens. At seven in the morning in mid-March, the sun had not yet come through the two narrow windows. In the yellow light from the single bulb, Yuki's red sweater and blue jeans looked unnaturally bright. Yuki did not look up from the magazine she had been reading in the dark. On the floor by her chair were her suitcase and the violets she had dug up by the river. Packed in plastic bags with air holes, the flowers reminded Masa of butterflies in a jar, their colors faded as though they had turned into bits of paper.

"Up so early? The first bus won't be here for two hours yet," Masa said.

"I know." Yuki took off the mittens and put them on the table.

"Do you want breakfast?"

"No."

Masa went to the sink all the same and measured the rice and water into a saucepan, filled the tin kettle, and placed them side by side on the burners. The house still smelled of the incense from yesterday when the priest

73

came to offer prayers for the third anniversary of her daughter Shizuko's death. Only three years, Masa thought, and already Yuki acts as if she's forgotten her mother and wants to forget us, too.

She sprinkled a handful of tea leaves into the kettle and sat down opposite Yuki, who continued to read the magazine. On the table next to the magazine, Yuki's yellow mittens looked awkward and crooked, one much larger than the other. Yuki had said that she had made them in a homemaking class at school. Masa wondered why she needed mittens in mid-March. It was warm outside; there were spring mums and early strawberries in the yard, violets and clover by the river.

Yesterday afternoon while the guests were arriving for the ceremony, Yuki went out in her black dress to dig up the violets by the river. She came into the house with soiled hands; by then, the priest was already burning the incense. She had washed her hands and sat through the ceremony, her back absolutely rigid, her posture too perfect. Her face had shown no grief or regret, while the others, some of them not even relatives, had pressed their handkerchiefs discreetly to their eyes during the priest's chanting. Now all the guests were gone and Masa was alone with Yuki. Her husband, Takeo, was still asleep.

"Are you sure you don't want breakfast?" Masa asked the second time.

"I'm sure," Yuki said, keeping her eyes on the magazine.

"If you don't like rice, I can borrow bread from the neighbors and make some toast."

"I'm not hungry."

"You'll be starved by the time you are on the train,"

Masa said. It was an hour's bus ride from her village into the city of Himeji, and then a three-hour train ride from there to Yuki's house in Kobe. Shizuko used to make that long trip every summer with Yuki. She called it "coming home" rather than "visiting." "Yuki and I are coming home as soon as her school's out," she would say. Every summer back then, Yuki did something that the neighbors in the village would talk about for months. Masa thought of the afternoon Yuki had climbed up the chestnut tree and been too frightened to come down. The firemen from a nearby town had come and spread a net under the tree for her to jump into. Then there was the morning when Yuki had run clear through the glass screen chasing a dragonfly. She had come through with small scratches and cuts on one side of her face, her arms and knees, but nothing serious, nothing that had to be stitched up later, and in any case, she had continued running until she caught the dragonfly. And for days she bragged about having more scars than anyone she knew, just as she had bragged the year before about being the only child in the village to jump into the firemen's net. That was Yuki as a child— cheerful and talkative. Everyone loved her in spite of the trouble she often caused. But she had changed, Masa thought; she had become quiet and moody. Masa had not seen her since her father's remarriage.

Masa took two thousand-yen bills out of her wallet and laid them on the table next to the mittens.

"You'll want to have lunch on the train," she said to Yuki.

"I don't plan to and if I do, I have enough money anyway. Lunches on trains don't cost this much."

"Then you can buy something else when you get back to Kobe. Get new mittens for next winter."

"I like these mittens. I told you I made them myself."

"They're too large for you."

"I like them this way. Tight mittens cut off my blood circulation. Besides, *she* said she would buy me new gloves and I told her I didn't want any. I couldn't buy new ones with your money after that."

"So she's good to you?" Masa asked.

"Of course she's good to me. What else do you expect? But what I like best about her is that she lets me do things on my own. I don't like to be coddled. I like to be on my own." Yuki paused and stared Masa right in the eyes. "And she and Father get on well. I think he's happier now than he's been in a long time."

Masa stood up and took the saucepan off the stove. She dished the first spoonful of rice into a small white cup used for the family altar and poured the tea into another. She placed the two cups on a tray and turned to Yuki.

"Why don't you take these to the altar?" she said. "You should burn another stick of incense and tell the spirits of our ancestors that you've come to say good-bye."

"I'd rather not." Yuki closed her magazine and looked up. "There's no one to say good-bye to."

Masa stared for a moment at the photograph of a model on the magazine cover. She was dressed in a red ski jacket and black pants. A tall foreign boy stood next to her, his large hand on her waist. The photograph looked flat, like a painted image.

"You shouldn't say things like that," Masa said.

"You'll anger the spirits and they won't watch over you anymore."

"You know as well as I do," Yuki retorted, "that the spirits of the ancestors, even if such things really existed, couldn't care less about whether I burn incense and tell them anything or not, and Mama, wherever she really might be, isn't in that little black box."

"Of course she isn't *in* the altar," Masa said. "But the altar is there so you can show respect for all the past members of our family who watch over you day and night. That includes your mother's spirit too, and you must show respect, especially for her."

"How can I respect someone who was cowardly enough to kill herself?" Yuki picked up the magazine and began to page through it quickly.

Before Masa could think of an answer, the kitchen door opened and Takeo appeared in his short brown kimono and long brown underwear. If he had heard Yuki's words, his face did not show it.

"What time does the bus come?" he asked.

"In less than two hours," Yuki said.

"Let's have breakfast," Takeo said. "There's plenty of time."

"Everybody's trying to make me eat," Yuki said. "Don't you see I'm just not hungry?"

"I'm going to the yard to pick some strawberries," Takeo said as if he hadn't heard. "Are you coming with me?"

"No. I don't want to eat them. And if you're going to make me eat them anyway, I'd rather not see them in the dirt. Maybe there are bugs on them."

"Suit yourself," Takeo said. "You don't have to see

77

the berries until I wash them and put them on your plate."

Masa watched him as he picked up a colander and walked out the back door from the kitchen. Then she took the tray and went to the family room, where the altar was, leaving Yuki alone in the kitchen with her magazines, mittens, and violets wrapped in plastic.

At the altar, Masa sat down and closed her eyes but could not pray. She thought instead of what Yuki had done on the morning before Shizuko's funeral: she had stood by the kitchen sink, washing her hair over and over. She had said that her hair first smelled of gas, and then of cigarette smoke, and then of incense, that these smells would never come out. Shortly before the funeral began, in the house filled with strangers, Masa came across her granddaughter in the narrow passageway by the kitchen. They embraced, and the water dripped from Yuki's hair onto Masa's shoulder. Masa could still remember the cold, wet circle that spread on the shoulder of her black kimono and lingered all afternoon.

My thoughts are troubled this morning. Grant me peace, Masa prayed to the spirits of her ancestors. She bowed her head and closed her eyes tighter.

After a while, she opened her eyes, collected the cups with yesterday's rice and tea, and replaced them. She lit a stick of incense and began to walk back to the kitchen. Already, the warm outside air was blowing into the house from the windows. It would be a humid spring day with a south wind. From the hallway, she saw a white flash of morning light as the back door swung open. Takeo's tall figure blocked the light. Masa suddenly remembered what he had written in his diary, the small black notebook with narrow black lines and

78

printed dates, on the day of Shizuko's death: *We are thankful for the peacefulness of her face.* It was such an obvious remark. Thankful for the peacefulness, Masa repeated to herself resentfully as she stepped into the kitchen—why did he say "we"?—it wasn't how she had felt at all; he had no business saying "we" without asking her. As she put the tray on the table, where Yuki was still reading her magazine, the bright red jacket in the photograph troubled her eyes. Masa reached toward the wall and flicked off the light. Sunlight was just beginning to stream into the windows. She blinked and looked toward the door just as Takeo tripped and began to fall forward. The colander flew from his hands, the strawberries scattering everywhere in a red blur. Masa started rushing toward him, but too late. Takeo hit the floor with a dull thump. The next moment, she and Yuki were both crouched over him. He lay on his stomach with his face turned aside.

"Grandpa." Yuki shook him by the shoulder. "Grandpa, are you all right?"

Takeo didn't open his eyes. His mouth was open slightly, and his breath made a faint wheezing sound.

Yuki was on her feet. She bent over and touched Masa's shoulder briefly. "Grandma," she said. "I'm going for the doctor. Wait for me." She dashed through the door, leaving it swinging, and sprinted down the dirt road away from the house.

Masa put her hand on her husband's neck. His skin was warm and wet from perspiration. His breathing made her hand move up and down, up and down. Takeo's face looked flushed and red. Masa reached under him and loosened the belt he wore around his kimono. She shook him gently, but he remained unconscious.

She ran to the hallway closet and returned with the first-aid kit. Kneeling over her husband, she opened the small black box. Inside, there was a jumble of bandages, cotton balls, tapes, bottles of Mercurochrome and peroxide, a pair of scissors. These are just for children, Masa thought; they're no use. Takeo had gotten the kit in town a few years back, and he was the one who used it to tend to the minor cuts and scratches their grandchildren got on their visits. I don't know what to do, Masa thought; I don't know how to help him.

She closed the box and put her hand on his neck again. His breathing seemed to have changed. He wasn't wheezing anymore, but breathing quietly. Maybe this is nothing, Masa thought. He'll wake up any moment now. But he didn't, and his breathing seemed to be slowing down. Masa got up and hurried to the bedroom.

Sitting down on the edge of the futon, she picked up the phone and then stopped. She didn't know the doctor's number. They hadn't called doctors in years. Unlike Yuki, the grandchildren who visited in recent years had no major accidents. Masa and her husband had never had anything but colds that went away on their own. She rummaged through the drawer for the phone book and opened it. The book had the numbers from all the neighboring villages arranged in some way she didn't understand. Finally, she found the doctor's number and dialed. His phone was busy. She waited a minute to try again, but the phone book had fallen shut. She couldn't recall the number. As she paged through the book again, her hands began to shake. Her heart was beating so fast it was hard to breathe. She imagined Takeo on the floor no longer breathing quietly but writhing in pain or choking. Her hands continued to shake as she dialed the number again.

"Hello," a woman's voice said. "Dr. Takeda's office."

"I need to speak with the doctor right away."

"I'm sorry. He just stepped out. Can he call you back?"

"No," Masa said. "This is an emergency. I need him right now. My husband is unconscious."

"Wait," the woman said. "This is Mrs. Matsumoto, right? The doctor just left to go to your house. Your granddaughter was here. They went on his motorcycle."

Masa let out the breath she had been holding. She swallowed hard. She was gripping the phone, and her palm was wet.

"Try and calm down, Mrs. Matsumoto," the woman was saying. "They should be there any minute. Just wait for them. Don't try to move him."

"All right," Masa managed to say. "I understand."

"Will you be okay yourself?" the woman asked. "Are you sitting down?"

Masa hung up without thinking and ran back to the kitchen. Takeo had rolled over onto his back. His eyes were open. She knelt down to touch his forehead. Just then, the back door swung open. Yuki and the doctor came in, both of them running. The doctor opened his bag and knelt on the other side of Masa. He was taking Takeo's pulse, listening to his heart. Takeo moved his head and leaned on one elbow.

"Don't sit up," the doctor said. "Lie still and take it easy." He continued to examine Takeo, feeling his legs and arms, listening again to his heart. Then he looked

81

back and motioned to Yuki, who was standing behind him. "Here, help me."

Together, the doctor and Yuki helped Takeo to his feet. They supported him between them, his arms around their shoulders. On the floor, the strawberries were everywhere, most of them crushed. "Easy," the doctor was saying. "Take it slow." Masa followed them into the bedroom. They laid Takeo on his futon. His eyes were open. He squinted at them and then opened his mouth.

"Don't worry, you're all right. You just fell down," the doctor said. "Here, someone get a glass of water."

Yuki ran to the kitchen and returned with a glass. The doctor put his arm behind Takeo's back and helped him sit up. "Drink all of it. You don't want to be dehydrated." He handed the glass to Takeo, who took it, his hands shaking a little.

Takeo finished the water. The doctor took the empty glass from him and handed it to Yuki, who set it aside.

"Now, lie back down," the doctor said, putting his arm behind Takeo and helping him ease back down on the futon. "You should try and sleep for a while. You need the rest."

Takeo closed his eyes. The doctor turned to Masa and Yuki. By then, Masa was sitting on the floor behind him, though she couldn't remember when she had sat down. She edged closer to Takeo's futon. Yuki reached out and held her hand.

"He'll be all right," the doctor said. "He must have gotten dizzy from stooping in the sun and getting up to walk too soon, then coming into the house where it's darker. It's a humid day. He should be careful in this kind of weather."

"He's not really hurt?" Yuki asked.

"No, I checked his arms and legs. He might have a few bruises, but nothing broken. No cuts or scratches. He's all right. Make sure he has some water to drink when he wakes up. I'll come back in a few hours to check on him again."

"Good," Yuki said. "Thank you."

Masa sat bolt upright, her hands and shoulders shaking. Yuki was still holding one of her hands. With her free hand, Yuki patted Masa's back as though she had been the one who was sick.

"I don't think it's anything very serious," the doctor was saying to Yuki. "But he should come in for a checkup." He turned to Masa. "Are you all right, Mrs. Matsumoto?" he asked. "You must have been frightened."

Masa nodded.

"You'd better take good care of your grandmother, too," the doctor said to Yuki as he got up.

"Thanks. I will," Yuki said. She stood up to show the doctor to the door.

Yuki returned with another glass of water and put it next to Takeo's futon. He was sleeping now, his face a little flushed, but his breathing easy and even. Yuki and Masa sat on the floor across from each other, leaning over Takeo.

"I'm going to call home," Yuki said. "I should tell them that I'm taking the afternoon bus and train instead. I don't want to leave until Grandpa wakes up and I can talk to him." She paused. "I forgot about the phone when I saw Grandpa fall. It was like when I was in grade school and you didn't have a phone. I ran all the way to the doctor's."

"It was as well," Masa said. "He was here so soon. I almost forgot about the phone too. By the time I tried to call him, you were already on your way."

"I told him it was an emergency. He took his motorcycle and made me ride on the back. I think I kept screaming in his ear. My throat feels scratchy." Yuki touched the edge of Takeo's futon. "When he was leaving just now, the doctor told me that in the three years he hadn't seen me, I had come to look more like Mama. He said I was lucky, Mama was so beautiful. He also asked me if I still chased dragonflies and ran into glass screens." She looked at her watch. "I'd better go call. Then I'm going to pick more strawberries. The doctor and I stepped all over the ones Grandpa picked. You want some, don't you?"

Masa nodded, but Yuki had already sprung to her feet and gone out of the room. Masa sat and watched Takeo sleeping. He had fallen forward just when she had been angry at him about his diary entry, almost as though her resentment had tripped him. Masa put her hand on his forehead, which was comfortably cool now. I am sorry, she thought. I know you've suffered too. You were picking strawberries for Yuki because you wanted to cheer her up. She moved the water glass closer so he could reach it easily and walked back to the kitchen.

In the kitchen, now bright with morning light, Yuki was washing the strawberries under the faucet. Masa went and stood beside her at the sink.

"I'll take the two o'clock bus," Yuki said. "Maybe Grandpa will wake up before then. If not, I'll leave even later." She stopped the faucet and turned to Masa.

In the sink, half of the strawberries were drying in the colander; the other half, with their stems, floated in a large wash basin. "I was scared that Grandpa would never speak again." She dipped her hands in the basin.

Masa nodded.

"I want to tell you something," Yuki said, her fingers moving the strawberries around in the water. "It's about Mama." She glanced at Masa a moment and then looked down at the strawberries. "The afternoon Mama died, I went to my piano lesson after school, like I always did on Wednesdays. Miss Uozumi was late, so her mother let me into their house and asked me to wait. I called Mama to tell her that I was going to be later than usual. It must have been right before she was going to do it." Yuki paused. "Would you rather if I didn't talk about this?" Her hands continued to swim in the water among the strawberries.

"It's all right. Go on," Masa said. Her throat felt tight.

"She sounded kind of strange over the phone," Yuki said. "Just before she hung up, she said, 'Be good. You know I love you.' I could still hear her voice saying that. It was something she might have said on any other day. It's just the way she said it, like she meant it for more than that one afternoon. It bothered me, the way she said it. But I didn't go home right away. You know, I even thought about it."

"You shouldn't blame yourself," Masa said. She knew about regrets. Even now, she stayed awake some nights feeling that she should have prevented her daughter's death, although she could never think of how.

"I don't blame myself," Yuki said. "Not really. Maybe I would have been too late even if I had left Miss Uozumi's house then. I know Mama meant to do what she did. If it wasn't that day, it might have been another time. But what bothers me is something else. When I got home, Mama was unconscious. Soon, she was turning cold. Father came home with the doctor in about a half hour, but she never spoke again. So I had been listening to her voice over the phone but not seeing her. And then a few hours later, I was seeing her body but no voice ever came again. It's like I can't remember her whole." Yuki pulled her hands slowly out of the water. "I remember her voice without her body and her body without her voice. Sometimes, I dream that her voice has been trapped in the telephone line somewhere, and I try but I can't help her. I just can't help her." She stared at her hands. "I wanted so much to help her." She shook her head and covered her face with her hands, her fingers pressing hard against her eyes.

Masa fumbled for a towel and handed it to Yuki. "I'm sorry," she said. "I'm sorry, Yuki."

Yuki wiped her face with the towel and looked up. Her eyes were red. "But I didn't tell you all this so you'd feel sorry for me. What I started to say was that *I* was sorry." She dropped the towel on the counter and rubbed her eyes with her knuckles. "When I saw Grandpa fall, I thought I might never hear his voice again, just like I won't hear Mama's. And I had been so awful to him and to you."

Yuki turned away from Masa toward the window. Her shoulders were shaking. Masa remembered the tight feeling in her stomach as she had stood in the yard and watched the small child fall from the chestnut tree into the firemen's net—and the moment when, frozen in helplessness, she had watched the same child run through the glass screen.

"I've been so awful," Yuki said, turning back to Masa, "ever since Mama died. I don't know why. It's like I just can't stop being that way. Everything seems so terrible, I don't know what to do except be awful myself. I'm sorry I said that Mama was a coward. But some days, I'm angry at her. I know she didn't mean to hurt me. She thought I would be better off without her, somehow. She was wrong. Still, she loved me. I know that, but it's hard." Yuki took a deep breath. "I get mad at everything and everyone, even you. I don't know what for. But I do love you and Grandpa. I think of you all the time in Kobe and miss you. Do you believe me?"

"Of course I do," Masa said. She put her hand on Yuki's back. "I do."

Masa drew her closer. Yuki leaned fiercely into her shoulder and hugged her tight. "I'm so sorry, Grandma," she said, her voice muffled. "I'm so sorry."

"It's all right," Masa said. "It's all right. I understand." As Masa patted Yuki's back, she could feel the hard bones under her T-shirt. Yuki had always been very thin. Masa remembered how small she had looked standing on one of the top branches of the chestnut tree with her arms wrapped around the thick trunk while the firemen were telling her to walk out to the end of the branch and jump. "I can't move," she had said at first. "I'm too scared." Then finally, she teetered to the end of the branch and stepped out into the clear space with nothing below her. It must have felt like a long fall toward the safety of the net. Masa closed her eyes and held her tighter. Yuki's cheek was warm against her shoulder and her hair smelled of sunlight and early spring.

8
Grievances
(May 1973)

Because the doctor's appointment had been in the morning, Yuki's stepmother, Hanae, was unable to begin cleaning the house until one o'clock. As always, she started in the kitchen. After she swept and mopped the floor, she polished the stove, the refrigerator, the table, the cabinet. It was important to clean every day. Overnight, dust accumulated on all horizontal surfaces. Fingerprints smudged the refrigerator door because her husband, Hideki, and her stepdaughter, Yuki, never learned to hold the door handle with their fingers curled in rather than spread out.

Some women, she thought as she proceeded to the bathroom, let their houses get dirty for two, three weeks before they got around to cleaning. Yuki's mother, Shizuko, must have been that kind of woman. When Hanae married Hideki three years ago, Yuki was already thirteen. Yet she had not been instructed in the proper ways to clean the house, to wash the dishes, to write up a shopping list.

"Whatever did your mother teach you?" Hanae had asked her once.

"She taught me things you wouldn't know about," Yuki had said. "She taught me to draw and paint. She

89

taught me the names of flowers and stories to tell from memory. She knew things no one else knew."

"She has not taught you good manners, it seems."

"No. What do I want with good manners? Why should I pretend to be nice to people when they don't like me and I don't like them? It's not honest."

Yuki had then looked her right in the eyes, something most children were taught never to do.

Hanae knelt down and ran her fingers over the bathroom floor to pick up the strands of hair that accumulated every day. They were too fine for the broom; wet rags made them stick harder to the tiles. Most of the hair, Hanae saw, was Yuki's. It was much blacker than her own, each strand almost twice as thick and shiny. Yuki had never been taught to brush her hair properly—with even strokes that made the loose strands collect between the bristles. During their first month together, Hanae had been sickened by the sight of long, tangled hair, in the bathroom, the hallway, even the kitchen. It was a good thing Yuki had cut her hair very short since then.

After flushing the hair down the toilet, Hanae went back to the kitchen for her bucket and rag. She stopped by the cabinet and squinted at the persimmon belly of the teapot. Six round cups and saucers were arranged in a circle around the pot.

Hanae had thrown out and replaced everything else in the kitchen to avoid cooking and serving with another woman's plates and utensils. Her husband had come home just as she was cramming this tea set into a box to carry to the dump.

He had looked at the china for a long time, hesitating.

Finally, he said, "Were you going to throw these away?"

"Would I pack them like this for any other purpose?"

"Maybe you should save them. They were her best tea set."

He frowned slightly as he said this, never mentioning his dead wife by name. Hanae made no comment.

"Good pottery like this should be passed on as heirlooms," Hideki said. "From mother to daughter. You could put them away if you don't want to see them yourself."

Hanae ripped open the box and put the large teapot back on the shelf, not saying a word. She made a point of arranging the cups and saucers around it exactly as they had been.

"You needn't display them in the cabinet," Hideki said. "Why don't you put them in the attic, where you wouldn't have to see them?"

Hanae turned her back to him and began to polish the glass doors of the cabinet. Hideki gave up and went back to his study.

The attic was already full of one thousand worthless things saved for Yuki. Hanae remembered the first time she went up there, at the end of her first day's cleaning. She had simply stood in the middle of the attic and stared. First, there were three wooden boxes of the dead woman's clothes. But that wasn't all. Other boxes were stacked up along every wall. Each had a label written in a neat feminine handwriting, undoubtedly the dead woman's: *Yuki's Baby Clothes*, *Yuki's Childhood Toys*, *Yuki's Crayon Sketches*, *Yuki's Music Books*, *Yuki's Essays*, *First Through Third Grade*, *Yuki's Watercolors*, *Fifth and Sixth Grades*. Since that first time, Hanae had gone back twice hoping to throw out one thing or another, but each time, she came down without accomplishing a thing. There were so many boxes she didn't know where to start. It was irritating to see Yuki's name repeated in the woman's handwriting, see the order in which everything had been arranged, the logic of it. Hanae couldn't stay in the attic for more than five minutes without thinking of the eight long years she herself had spent seeing Hideki only in secret. All that time, the woman had had a house to herself, an attic to fill up with all the silly things she felt like saving. The thought made her so angry that soon Hanae gave up the idea of cleaning the attic and avoided going there at all. Some mornings, though, while she cleaned the rest of the house so it was spotless, Hanae felt suffocated by the thought of the dust in the attic above her. The house never felt completely clean. She would go back to all the rooms twice or three times to check every corner. Finding a dustball underneath a bookcase where she had just spent ten minutes cleaning, she could almost see how it had descended from the attic and crept underneath her furniture as soon as her back was turned. Her head spun with rage.

The tea set had remained in the cabinet because Hanae was not going to add to the dead woman's collection of things in the attic to be saved for Yuki. Besides, she could not put it out of her sight after her husband had made such a feeble, awkward attempt at saving her feelings—repeating twice that she need not see it herself, as though the dead woman's tea set might cause her to have any special feelings. That was ridiculous. After all, it was just a pile of old pottery. Still, seeing it again this afternoon made Hanae feel as though a piece of metal was lodged in her rib cage.

She turned away from the cabinet, grabbed the bucket and the rag, and went back to the bathroom. As she knelt on the floor and squeezed the rag, her knuckles went white and sweat poured down her back. She was thinking about the doctor again.

He had told her that she would never have a child.

"I'm afraid," he had said, hesitating as though he was embarrassed, "that it's too late. You should have come to see me when your periods became so infrequent."

"But that was six years ago," Hanae had said. "I couldn't have had a child back then. I didn't know I would ever be in a position to have his child."

The doctor looked away in clear embarrassment. He knew that six years ago, Hanae had not been married.

As water poured back from the rag into the bucket, Hanae thought of Hideki. Why hadn't he let her have a child back then? He was already making enough money to help her quit her secretarial job and have his child. Many men with his income had done that rather than divorcing their wives and causing scandals. They kept a second household. It was a perfectly acceptable alternative. Hideki was wrong, Hanae thought, in not having offered her this chance six or seven years ago, when they had been lovers for over two years. Even back then, he could have seen that Shizuko might someday commit suicide. To do such a thing, she must always have been unstable, strange. Why couldn't he have seen that her life might end in just such a way, leaving him to marry again?

Instead, he had kept their affair a secret. When Hanae began to miss her periods, he was worried at first that she might be pregnant. He sent her to a clinic in Waka-yama, two hours by train, to find out. He didn't want anyone in town to know in case she was pregnant. But month after month, the test was negative. Soon, he wasn't worried anymore. When she suggested going to a doctor to see if anything was wrong, he said not to worry, she was perfectly healthy. She had believed him. He had allowed her to turn into a barren woman.

"There must be something I can still do," Hanae said to the doctor. "People take medications for that, don't they, to be able to have children?"

"I couldn't recommend that for you, Mrs. Okuda. Treatments like that could take years, and there's no guarantee that they would work. It might have been dif-ferent, had you been younger. But you're thirty-six and you've never been pregnant. I'm sure any other doctor will tell you the same thing. Let it be."

To her chagrin, Hanae had started crying right in the doctor's office.

"I'm sorry," the doctor said. "I suppose you wanted to give your husband a son."

Hanae gritted her teeth to stop her crying.

"If it's any consolation," the doctor went on, "most people nowadays think that a daughter is just as good. Especially in Mr. Okuda's case. I hear that his daughter is exceptionally bright. My girl, you see, goes to the same school as your stepdaughter. She's a year younger. She really admires Miss Okuda. Last year, when Miss Okuda became the president of her class for the second time, my girl talked of nobody else."

Everyone admired Yuki—so bright, so talented. Hanae was sick of the compliments—compliments that implied that she was fortunate to have such an exceptional stepdaughter. Above all, she was sick of not being able to contradict them. She had to thank the admirers with a smile and never let on that she and Yuki hardly spoke to each other.

She had thanked the doctor as best she could and hurried out of the office.

As she continued to clean the rest of the downstairs—the bedroom, the living room, Hideki's study—she couldn't help repeating in her mind the things that had most annoyed her in the last three years. When she was going up the stairs to clean the rest of the house, she became aware of the dull pain in her jaw and realized that she had been clenching her teeth.

By the time she went into Yuki's room, it was past four thirty. She always saved Yuki's room for last, just before she swept down the stairway, mopped the downstairs hallway the second time, and put away her broom, bucket, and rags, all of them thoroughly cleaned.

As usual, Yuki's room was clean. The desk top was free of the books and paper she used to leave scattered all over it. Hanae could see that Yuki had dusted the shelves before she went to school. The floor, too, was clear of the clothes and books she used to leave there. Yuki had cleaned the carpet with the small vacuum cleaner kept in the hallway closet. She did this every morning before going to school not because she wanted to learn to clean properly, Hanae felt, but to keep her out of the room as much as possible. Hanae tried the desk drawers. As always, they were locked. Yuki must be keeping the keys in her schoolbag. No matter how carefully she looked through the room, Hanae could never find them.

"It's unhealthy how she locks up everything," she had complained to her husband. "Your daughter's growing up to be a close, sly person."

Hideki had said nothing. He did not deny that it was unhealthy, but he did not offer to do anything about it. That was what she hated most about him—he did nothing to discipline Yuki. It wasn't that he took her side. Trying to save the tea set was the only thing he ever did for her. But even that, he must not have done really to please his daughter. As far as Hanae knew, he never told Yuki that he was saving the tea set for her. Instead, he avoided her altogether. He did not exchange more than a few words with her every week, and those few words he managed came out of absolute necessity. This, Hanae knew, was not as it should be. If he were a better husband, he would interfere on her behalf and exercise his authority over his unruly daughter. Instead, he thought only of his own convenience and avoided her.

Hanae walked away from the neatly cleaned desk and correctly made bed toward the closet. She opened the closet door and finally found something Yuki had not done properly.

The closet was full of the old summer clothes she had told Yuki to throw out—skirts that were too short, dresses whose patterns were too childish, blouses with too many frills and embroidered flowers. Yuki had grown taller in the last three years but stayed so thin that she was able to wear most of these old clothes. Still, they made her look ridiculous. They had all been made by her mother when Yuki was in grade school. At the end of last summer, Hanae had told her to take them to the garbage dump. Some of the skirts were so short that they exposed her bony kneecaps. People would see her dressed this way and know that Hanae and Yuki did not get along. They would say that Hanae, a horrible stepmother, let her stepdaughter go about in rags. Hanae's hands sweated at this thought. It was unfair. Every year, she went out by herself and bought Yuki sensible clothes she did not need to try on—white blouses, black or blue skirts, brown and gray pants with elastic waists, all of them long and roomy enough to last her a few years even if she continued to grow. None of them had been put out. The only new clothes on the hangers were the things Yuki had bought for herself with the money she made last summer shelving books at the city library. They were ridiculously bright cotton dresses made in India, T-shirts with rainbows or flowers painted on them. Hanae grimaced at them. Still, many girls Yuki's age wore such clothes. The neighbors would think nothing of her wearing them. But all the handmade clothes should go.

Taking a deep breath, Hanae began to rip the clothes off the hangers. The large, sweeping motions of her own arms soothed her so that her breathing became a little easier as she continued. When she was done, she bundled them firmly under her right arm and squeezed them hard, feeling nothing but contempt. Yuki's mother must have spent hours embroidering flowers on these dresses and blouses to be worn only by a little girl, a good-for-nothing tomboy at that. No wonder her husband stayed away. As she sat alone night after night, sadness and craziness must have accumulated in her mind like dust, till her clogged-up mind made her turn on the gas in an empty house and suffocate to death.

Clutching the old clothes, Hanae began to descend

the stairway. The bundle blocked her vision. She had to be careful not to lose her footing.

She was so absorbed in not missing the steps that she did not hear the door open. Halfway down the stairs, she noticed Yuki standing in the doorway, staring at her. Yuki had put down her school things on the floor. Hanae thought of the dust or dirt she might have tracked in. Dirt sometimes clung to the bottom of her bag and was carried into the house.

"Please don't take them away," Yuki said. "They're all I have left. You've thrown out my winter clothes already and everything else."

"I have no idea what you're talking about," Hanae said. "These clothes are too short and childish for you. You might have considered what people would say about me if you went around looking like a little beggar girl."

"I won't wear them then. Let me at least save them."

"What for? They're absolutely useless."

"You know my mother made them for me. They're all I have left now." Yuki covered her face with her hands.

Hanae stood on the stairway, looking down at her. She had seldom seen her cry. Many mornings, though, Yuki came down with her eyelids all puffed up, and Hanae despised her for crying in bed. Even her crying, it seemed, was secretive. She was doing her best to suppress it now.

"You are a close, sly girl, Yuki. Why must you pretend that I'm such a horrible stepmother? I buy you clothes every year. You go about pretending that I don't even do that much of my duty."

"I pretend nothing," Yuki said. "You are the one who

pretends. When other people are around, you pretend that you like me. You pretend that we're all happy together. I don't pretend. I hate you."

Yuki was coming up the stairs slowly.

Hanae remembered her wedding. She could still see Yuki's hands bringing down the bowl of sake against the tabletop. Her knees felt weak.

"You must give me back my clothes," Yuki said, looking Hanae right in the eyes. She was only a few steps below her now. The wedding bowl had broken up into small, jagged pieces, and the pungent smell of sake had spread through the room.

Yuki took another step and reached out her hand. Hanae flinched and almost lost her balance. For a moment, they were both looking at the clothes in Hanae's arms. When their eyes met again, Hanae leaned forward and gave Yuki a hard push.

Hanae screamed. Oh, she thought to herself, she would have killed me if I hadn't pushed her just in time; there was madness in her eyes.

Yuki lost her balance and began tumbling down the steps, but somehow she managed to grab hold of the banister and break her fall. She slid down a few more steps and stopped. Slowly, she moved her hands and feet until she was kneeling on the steps and leaning against the wall. Her hand was curled tight around her right ankle. She said nothing. She just looked at Hanae.

"You almost hurt me, Yuki," Hanae said. "You would have pushed me down the stairs."

"You pushed me down."

Neither said a word for a while.

Then suddenly, Yuki leaned her head against the wall and began to cry. Her shoulders were heaving up and down, choked-up moans escaping her mouth. She didn't even cover her face with her hands as most girls would. She did nothing to restrain the gasping noise of her breaths.

There, Hanae thought, again was a sign of violent temper, craziness. Someday Yuki would become as crazy as her mother had been. She could already predict what kind of end Yuki's life might come to.

Cautiously, Hanae descended the stairs. Yuki was leaning hard into the wall. There was just enough room for her to pass by.

As Hanae inched past her, Yuki suddenly stopped crying.

"Don't worry," she said, her voice harsh and low. "I won't tell Father about how you tried to push me down the stairs. He won't believe me. But I'll never forget it myself."

"I didn't push you, really. You fell down while you leaned forward and tried to push me."

"That's a lie and you know it. Your whole life is a lie."

Yuki began to climb up the stairs, not turning back toward Hanae once. She walked painfully, as though she was trying not to limp.

Hanae heard her go into her room and shut the door. She didn't slam it as any other girl might have done. She shut it quietly, deliberately. Hanae climbed down the last steps. Yuki had left her bag and books by the door. They were scattered about in a most disorderly way. Yuki had no sense of keeping her books neat. Their pages were bent, their covers scratched. As she watched the things Yuki had left, Hanae felt a sharp wedge inside her chest. She squeezed her arms hard around the old clothes and walked out the door to the shed. There, she crammed the clothes in a battered cardboard box. They would stay there till the next garbage day, becoming infested with spiders and moths.

Hanae went inside the house. She walked directly to the kitchen and stopped in front of the cabinet. The wedge inside her chest grew sharper. She opened the glass door and gathered all the persimmon-colored pieces into her arms. The cups and saucers clattered against each other in the crook of her elbow. She took them to the sink, set them down on the counter, and shattered them one by one. The broken pieces filled the sink while Hanae counted her grievances against the living and the dead.

9
Homemaking
(November 1973)

Cooking the rice was Yuki's responsibility. With her hand, she stirred the raw grains in the pan of cold water, exactly twenty-five times. The powdery white coating came off and clouded the water. She drained the pan and measured the correct amount of water into it. The other girls in her group were peeling and cutting up the vegetables. She watched the girl nearest her cut open a green pepper and scrape the seeds and white membranes into the garbage pail. As always, her group was the slowest. The other five teams already had their rice cooking, their vegetables cut up. They were mixing the tempura batter and heating the oil for deep frying.

The homemaking class met the hour before lunch. The teacher, Miss Sakaki, made each group set a table and eat in the classroom-kitchen during the lunch recess. The students then had just enough time to wash the dishes and run to their fifth-hour classes. Today in Yuki's fifth-hour class, they would dissect frogs. That thought and the smell of grease made her sick to her stomach.

She had tried to get out of the dissection. She had talked to the biology teacher, Mr. Wada, while he was straightening out his desk after class the day before.

"I don't want to dissect the frog," she had said to him.

"Why? Are you afraid?"

"No. I don't think it's right to take things apart when you already know what's inside them. There's no point. Look." She opened her textbook to the color photograph of a frog under dissection. "I already know this is what I'll find inside. I don't have to cut one open."

"Last year in your sophomore class, you dissected an earthworm and an oyster," Mr. Wada said. "You didn't have any problems then, did you? Those things were alive. The frogs will be dead when you get them."

"That makes no difference. Besides, I shouldn't have dissected those other things last year."

"Why not?"

Yuki couldn't answer. She remembered the oyster, a shell the size of a wristwatch. She had pried it open as casually as if it were a machine she could put together again. Inside, the flesh was soft and wet. The small parts she sliced away and identified already smelled of decay.

"You're not bothered about killing earthworms and frogs, are you?" Mr. Wada asked her. "I always thought that students enjoyed the dissections once they got over their squeamishness."

She thought about the earthworm, the way her scalpel had sliced it neatly in two, its outer skin turning transparent, almost beautiful.

"But that's what's wrong," she said. "Our enjoying it. I realized it's wrong to cut open something and enjoy it. Especially when there's no need to because we already know what's inside."

"I'm sorry you have gotten to be a high school junior

103

without learning to enjoy the scientific process. To me, that has been the most important thing, the process of learning. I'm disappointed. I always thought you were a good student."

Yuki had nothing more to say.

"Be sure you don't skip the lab," Mr. Wada said. "If you don't come for the dissection, you'll have to make it up some other time by yourself."

He had turned his back and walked out of the room, giving her no choice. She had been thinking about the dissection for a whole day now. Even the cut-up green peppers reminded her of the frogs.

Miss Sakaki was standing at their table.

"Let's not dawdle," she said. "Yuki, the rice doesn't have to soak for the rest of the hour."

Yuki took the pan out of the sink and put it on the gas stove. Miss Sakaki was inspecting the cut vegetables. Yuki struck several matches before the fire caught. She held her breath to avoid the smell of gas. She felt dizzy.

"You have to hold the match close enough for the fire to catch. Didn't I tell you that several times?" Miss Sakaki said.

Yuki looked away and pretended not to hear.

"Now the fire's too strong. Turn it down. I'm speaking to you, Yuki." Miss Sakaki's voice was loud enough for the whole class to hear. Several girls turned away from their tasks to look at Yuki. Their glances seemed sympathetic.

The first time the class had met, at the beginning of the second term in September—almost two months ago now—Miss Sakaki had divided them into six groups and instructed them to bake various kinds of cupcakes. The cupcakes Yuki's group made overflowed in the oven. Through the glass door, they could see the batter bubbling up and spreading. Some of it started trickling down to the broiler. Yuki took out her sketchbook and began to sketch the overflowing batter. She was just finishing it when Miss Sakaki took out the pan and slammed the oven shut.

"How irresponsible can you be? Don't you see it was ruining the pan and the oven?" Miss Sakaki said, addressing only Yuki. When the batter hardened, the pan looked like the craters of the moon. Yuki took it to her advanced painting class. She painted the ruined pan against the background of a perfectly set table and called it *Homemaking*. Her art teacher hung the painting in the hallway where he displayed the best work by his students every term. Miss Sakaki told Yuki's group to come back after school to bake another batch of cupcakes before the three-week unit was over. Yuki didn't go because she had cross-country practices after school. She got an *F* for the unit. Now everyone in the class agreed that Miss Sakaki had a special dislike for Yuki.

Miss Sakaki was walking away toward the center of the room. While Yuki was watching her, the rice began to boil over. She turned down the burner sharply. The flame went out and the smell of gas stung her nostrils. Without turning off the burner, she quickly struck a match and thrust it as close to the metal ring as possible. The flame almost burned her fingertips.

Miss Sakaki clapped her hands several times.

"Look over here a moment, class," she said. She held up a picture of a table setting. It showed a large white platter filled with tempura-fried vegetables and decorated with bamboo leaves and yellow chrysanthemums.

"Presentation of the food is as important as its taste,"

Miss Sakaki said as she put down the book. "Color is a vital factor. What you are making today—tempura and rice—will be very dull in color, just brown and white. So we have to think of how we can make it look appealing. I want one of you to go outside to the woods behind the gym and gather enough leaves, flowers, or berries for all of us. Then each group will arrange its own platter. This project will be graded on the presentation as well as the food itself. Now, who would like to volunteer?"

"Let me go," Yuki said, so loudly that everyone in the class looked at her.

Miss Sakaki frowned. No one else raised her hand.

"Will someone else volunteer?" Miss Sakaki said. "Yuki, I don't think you should go. You have so much to learn in the kitchen yet. I want to send someone who can already cook."

Still, nobody else volunteered. They were all watching Yuki.

"You have to let me go," Yuki said. "I feel dizzy. I could use some fresh air. It would be unkind of you not to let me go."

Miss Sakaki was silent.

"Please let her go," a girl who stood near Miss Sakaki said suddenly. "She'll be good with colors, don't you think? She's an artist. Besides, she can get to the woods and back faster than any of us. She runs faster than any other girl in the whole city."

"Yes," another girl said. "If you send someone else, our tempura could be stone cold before they come back."

A ripple of laughter went through the class.

"You have to let me go," Yuki said again.

Miss Sakaki stood pursing her lips for a while. Then she said, "You must come back within ten minutes. If you are not back in ten minutes, I can't give you credit for the meal."

One of the girls in her group handed her a white colander. Yuki took it and ran out of the kitchen.

Yuki stood on the edge of the woods and gathered red Japanese maple leaves into her colander. Since the leaves that had fallen to the ground were dry and brown, she snipped the bright red leaves off the branches. Each leaf, smaller than a child's hand, had a perfect webwork of veins.

About an hour northeast of Kobe by car was a mountain famous for its maple trees and wild monkeys. When Yuki was ten, she went there with her mother in mid-October and walked on the mountain paths. All around them and above them, wild monkeys screeched among the blazing red leaves. Yuki felt as though she and her mother were walking through fire without being burned. At the bottom of the mountain, an old man was selling maple leaves dipped in batter and lowered for a brief second into the hot oil in his portable cooker. Yuki had never heard of eating maple leaves. She and her mother shared a plate of them, all the time trying to describe to each other what they tasted like. Finally, her mother said, "It's like eating air, delicious mountain air." "Or maybe a wind," Yuki said. "I'm eating a south wind."

As she continued to snip the leaves, Yuki wondered if she would be better at homemaking if her mother was still alive. During the first term, when all the junior girls had to take sewing from another homemaking teacher, several of her friends smuggled their sewing out of the classroom in their knapsacks. When the class met the next time, their crooked stitches were straightened out, their tangled threads untangled and wound neatly around the bobbins. Her friends had gotten their mothers to help, though all of them complained about their mothers very often. "My mother is too old-fashioned," one of them would say. "Mine too," another would add. "She gets angry if I come home after nine, but lets my brothers stay out until eleven." "That's nothing," the first one would say. "My mother and I had a big fight last night because I forgot to do the dishes. She said she won't help me with anything anymore since I didn't help her." Listening to their talk, Yuki wondered if she and her mother would have had similar fights. Maybe they would have. Still, she wouldn't have asked her mother for help and then criticized her the way her friends did. That was unfair. She would have tried to appreciate the good things about her mother. Her mother could have straightened out any of her crooked seams, untangled any knotted thread. She could have shown her how to treadle on the sewing machine without being distracted by the needle going up and down. Her mother had been very good at making things.

The bruise Yuki had gotten on the stairway in May when she tried to save her clothes from her stepmother had turned out to be a bad sprain. For two weeks, she had to swim laps in the pool instead of going to her track practice. She was given a lane to herself against the wall. Yuki had to close her eyes and turn her head when the boys on the swim team passed her. Often, she swallowed water and gagged. Every time that happened, she remembered falling down the stairs. She could see her stepmother's arm shoving at her. One afternoon, standing in the pool and coughing, Yuki decided to remember and draw the clothes her mother made for her. She was afraid that all the things that had happened to her in the last three years might crowd up her mind and erase her memories about her mother, the way you could record over something by mistake on a tape recorder.

From that day on, Yuki began making colored-pencil drawings of the clothes her mother had sewn and embroidered for her. She kept the sketchbook locked inside her desk. Working at her summer job at the city library, she had carried a small notebook in her back pocket to write down the things she might suddenly remember during the day. One afternoon, a dress she had forgotten about came flying out of nowhere into her memory while she was shelving books. It came to her with its ruby red sleeves open wide, the row of buttons shining down the front. She could hardly wait to go back to her room to draw it. When she was done with the clothes, she made sketches of the tea set, the glazed plates, the white goblets, and the other pottery pieces that her stepmother had thrown out. Her friends and even her art teacher might laugh at her if she told them, but she didn't want to forget anything.

The colander was half full. Yuki looked at her watch. She had been gone for five minutes now. She thought it was unfair of Miss Sakaki to make her come back in ten minutes. If someone else had volunteered, Miss Sakaki wouldn't have been so strict. Even the fastest group would need at least twenty more minutes to prepare their food.

Yuki knelt down and scooped up handfuls of pine needles off the ground. Their smell reminded her of the delicious mountain air she and her mother had eaten. She put the pine needles on top of the maple leaves. There were three minutes left. Yuki got up and started to walk quickly past the gym toward the main building, careful not to spill the leaves.

The concrete path she was on wound around the biology lab at the southwest corner of the building. Yuki slowed down. From the window, she could see the jar of frogs on the teacher's desk. She stopped and veered off the path toward the outside wall of the lab. Standing among the prickly bushes planted thick against the building, she looked inside. The lab was empty, but the desk had already been prepared for the fifth-hour class. Along with the jar of frogs there were microscopes, scalpels, and scissors laid out in neat rows. From where she stood, she couldn't see the frogs closely. They were stacked up inside the jar. All she could see was their muddy brown color.

Yuki went along the wall, pushing at the windows. The fourth one slid up.

She put her colander through to the windowsill on the other side. Then, scratching her legs in the bushes, she clambered up and crawled through into the lab. She left the colander on the sill and went straight up to the desk.

There were at least twenty frogs in the jar. They were sprawled so closely on top of each other that she couldn't count them toward the bottom. Some were flattened against the glass. What she noticed most was how large they were. Each of them was larger than her fist.

She lifted the lid off the jar. The smell of formaldehyde gagged her.

It wasn't exactly the same smell that she remembered from her mother's funeral. Still, it reminded her of standing outside the crematorium while her mother's body was burned. Black smoke came out of the chimney and a sick, salty smell filled her lungs. Afterward, she had to go inside with a small group of relatives. The fire had shattered the bones. They were broken in bits, all of them as small as teeth. According to the Buddhist custom, the bones were gathered into a small urn, which would be kept in a temple. The others, all grownups, were completely silent as they picked the bones. Yuki tried to hold her breath as she grasped her long tongs. Her insides ached as though she was holding something that had sharp edges.

Even though the smell of the frogs was different, it choked her throat in the same way.

She put the lid down on the table and turned away to take a deep breath. Then, holding that breath, she picked up the jar with both hands and walked to the window she had come through.

The jar was heavy. She had to hurry. Her heart was pounding from the lack of air. She leaned out the window, flung out her arms, tipped the jar upside down and held it there. The dead frogs fell out of the jar into the space between the wall and the bushes. She put the jar back on the windowsill, breathed, and looked down. Nobody could see the frogs under the bushes. She was light-headed. Her chest hurt.

Her colander was still on the windowsill. Her eyes rested a moment on the bright red maple leaves, the slender curves of the pine needles.

111

Quickly, she took the empty jar to the nearest sink and turned on the faucet. The steam from the hot water made her face tingle. She washed the jar, dried it with a white apron that hung on the wall, and reached for the colander.

It was absolutely quiet in the hallway. If she hurried, no one would see her. She emptied the leaves into the jar. The smell of pine needles tickled her nose.

Moving silently, Yuki got the lid from the desk, washed and dried it, and put it back on the jar. The maple leaves and pine needles had filled the jar almost to the top. She placed the jar carefully in the center of the desk among the scalpels and microscopes. Then she took the empty colander and walked to the window, crawled through, and sat for a moment balanced on the edge, swinging her legs. She looked right and left. Nobody was in sight. First, she tossed the colander, which landed on the edge of the concrete path. The next moment, she pushed off with her arms and jumped out. She landed neatly on her two feet beyond the bushes and picked up the colander. Then, grasping it like a baton, she sprinted toward the woods for more maple leaves like clustered flames, pine needles that smelled of mountain air. Her ten minutes were long since used up. Miss Sakaki would fail her for today's assignment. Still, she would return in time to fill the tables with color. She began to smile as she ran.

10
The Golden Carp
(August 1974)

Her father was sitting in a black swivel chair at his desk. Yuki went into the study and stood behind him. He turned to her, holding out a white envelope by one corner.

"I was asked to give this to you," he said.

The envelope had her name on the front without an address. On the back, Yuki found her aunt Aya's name written in ink. Her heart beat a little faster. She had not seen Aya since her father's wedding. She waited for her father to dismiss her so she could go and read the letter, but he said nothing. He was frowning. His fingers kept tapping the arm of his chair.

"Is there anything else?" she asked him.

"Are you going to read the letter?"

"When I'm alone."

Her father sighed. "As you wish," he said.

She was about to turn around, to leave, when he added, "Your aunt put that letter inside her letter to me and sent it to my office."

Yuki nodded. Though she wrote to her aunt and her grandparents once a month, she never received letters from them. The only letter she had gotten from her mother's family in the last five years was a wedding invitation, two years ago, from her youngest uncle, Saburo. Her father had handed it to her at dinner, already opened. "Send him a telegram to congratulate him," he said. "Tell him you're sorry you can't attend. I'll give you the money." "No, thank you," Yuki said. "I'd rather write to him." Her stepmother put down her rice bowl. She said, "Be sure to show the letter to your father before you send it." "No," Yuki said. "I don't show my letters to anyone." Her stepmother got up and walked out of the kitchen then. She went to the living room and slammed the door. Her father waited a few minutes and followed her. Yuki went upstairs without finishing her dinner. He must have apologized to her stepmother, but he didn't insist on seeing Yuki's letter. He never mentioned it. Opening the invitation, Yuki concluded, was more her stepmother's idea than his.

"You don't have to read the letter in front of me or show it to me," he was saying now.

"Of course not," Yuki said. "Aunt Aya sealed the envelope and put my name on it because she meant it only for me."

"That's right," her father said. "But you don't have to be so angry about it."

Yuki said nothing.

"You should be happy," her father continued, "because your aunt is getting married and I'm letting you attend the wedding."

Yuki stood still, trying not to show her surprise.

Her father grasped the chair arms with both hands. "I know you blame me for not letting you go to your uncle's wedding," he said.

She shrugged. She had nothing to say.

"But I don't owe your uncle a favor. Your aunt Aya

is different. She took care of you for a year. I'm obligated to her because of that. I have to let you go to her wedding so our debts can be even and I won't owe her anymore. Do you understand?"

Yuki shrugged again. "I understand that's how you think about it."

Her father shook his head.

"May I go now?"

"The wedding will be in February," he said, "at your grandparents' house. You may stay there overnight."

Yuki looked back at her father from the doorway. "If I understand right," she said, "I don't have to thank you for letting me go. You are paying back my aunt rather than doing me a favor." She stepped out into the hallway without waiting for his answer.

As she closed the door of her room and sat down at her desk, she could hear her father leaving the living room and walking toward the kitchen. Soon, there were two voices—her stepmother's shrill nagging, her father's low mumble. Though she couldn't hear the words, they sounded like they were having an argument. Her stepmother must be upset because her husband was letting Yuki attend the wedding and he had not insisted on seeing her letter. Yuki waited until the voices stopped and then opened the envelope. The blue sheet inside was folded in three. She unfolded it slowly.

Yuki, her aunt had written in black ink. *I hope you are well. I look forward to your letters every month though I do not write back out of respect for your father's wishes. I am enclosing this letter in the one I'm sending him. I hope he will make an exception for once and let me see you.*

I am getting married in February to Mr. Kimura. I

*know you will remember him. We want you to be at the
wedding at your grandparents' house because we would
never have met if it had not been for you. You brought
us together that time Mr. Kimura came to my house to
see you after he heard about your mother. He and I
have gone on seeing each other since then, once every
month when he came to Tokyo to see his daughter. Now,
we have decided to be married. I will be moving back
to Kobe with him after our wedding.*

*I am very anxious to see you, as are your grandpar-
ents. I hope your father will decide to let you come, or
at least show you this letter. I want to see you face to
face and tell you much more.*

Be well. Your aunt, Aya.

Yuki read the letter over and then put it back into the
envelope. She locked the envelope into her desk and
then sat staring at the falling dusk.

Mr. Kimura, she thought; I can't believe it. And they
think it was because of me.

The first time Yuki saw Mr. Kimura, she was ten. It was
a Saturday in early June, almost at the end of the first
term of school. Yuki had spent the afternoon with her
neighbors, the Shirakawas, while her mother went to the
class reunion of her grade school. At dusk, Yuki was
sitting in the Shirakawas' kitchen when she heard a car
stop in front of her house. She said good-bye and ran
out to the street.

Instead of the shiny black cab she was expecting,
Yuki saw a small white car. Her mother was sitting next
to a man. They had turned off the headlights but the engine was still running. They were talking.

Yuki went up to the passenger's side and tapped on

the glass. Her mother turned to her and smiled. She was wearing a white linen dress and a lavender scarf. After the man cut off the engine, both of them stepped out of the car.

"How was your reunion, Mama?" Yuki asked, taking her mother's hand and swinging it back and forth.

"It was a lot of fun," she said. "Yuki, this is my friend Mr. Kimura. He and I went to school together. He gave me a ride home from downtown."

Mr. Kimura held out his hand. "Hi," he said as they shook hands. "It's very nice to meet you." He smiled, looking right into Yuki's face. She smiled back.

"Did you have a good afternoon?" her mother asked.

Yuki shrugged. "So-so," she said. "Mrs. Shirakawa started changing her baby's diaper in front of me. I was embarrassed, so I went in the other room."

"Oh, Yuki." Her mother was laughing. "Did you have dinner?"

Yuki shook her head. "No, I said I wasn't hungry."

"Why was that?"

"Mrs. Shirakawa was making some soup with oysters. I think maybe they were alive when she put them in the soup. She said she soaked them in water all day so they would spit out any sand they might have eaten."

"So you decided to skip dinner."

"I wasn't being rude. I wouldn't have eaten live oysters at anyone else's house either, so I wasn't insulting Mrs. Shirakawa in particular."

Her mother and Mr. Kimura glanced at each other. Mr. Kimura was trying not to laugh. His mouth kept wanting to turn up at the corners.

"What do you think?" Yuki asked him. "You don't think I was rude, do you?"

"No, no," Mr. Kimura said. "I probably wouldn't have eaten oyster soup either."

"See," Yuki said to her mother. "I'm going in the house to make myself a tomato and cheese sandwich. Can I make you one?"

"No, thank you. I had dinner at the reunion," her mother said.

"How about you?" Yuki asked Mr. Kimura. "Would you like a sandwich?"

"No. I also ate at the reunion. But thank you all the same."

Her mother looked at him and hesitated a second. Then she said, "Would you like to come inside and have some tea with us?"

"I would love to, but I don't want to intrude on your husband on a Saturday evening."

"My husband isn't home," her mother said.

"He doesn't come home till very late," Yuki added.

The three of them walked into the house in silence.

"So you are in fourth grade," Mr. Kimura said to Yuki while they were seated at the kitchen table.

Yuki put down her sandwich and nodded.

Mr. Kimura smiled at her mother. She tilted the teapot over his cup.

"When your mother and I were in fourth grade," Mr. Kimura said, "we stood side by side every morning at assembly because we were the shortest kids in our class."

"Really?" Yuki said. Even sitting down, Mr. Kimura was tall and thin. He was wearing a light green cotton shirt.

"I have grown since then." He laughed. "But in

fourth grade, your mother got me into trouble." He stopped a moment, nodded at Shizuko, and then continued. "Our fourth grade was a few years before the War. There was already a lot of talk about how our country should send soldiers to occupy China. At school, the principal made speeches about the greatness of our empire and unveiled the picture of the emperor. We were supposed to close our eyes and bow to the picture. The teachers told us that the emperor was so holy that even looking at his picture would blind us. But your mother didn't believe them. She looked at the picture one day, poked me in the elbow, and said, 'Look, he has such a funny nose.' Everyone heard her and assumed that I was looking too."

Her mother was smiling.

"Were you?" Yuki asked Mr. Kimura. "Were you looking?"

He shook his head. "No, I was a coward compared to your mother. I was afraid."

"It wasn't that I was brave," Shizuko protested. "I knew our teachers were lying to us. Someone, a photographer, must have taken the picture. Surely he had not lost his eyesight for that. So I wanted to prove the truth. That's why I looked. Still, I was surprised that the emperor looked so ordinary. Only, he had a funny, thin nose. If anything, he looked silly."

Mr. Kimura turned from Yuki to Shizuko. "I thought about you on the day the War ended, when the emperor made his speech on the radio and said he was only human, we were wrong to worship him. I was in high school by then and getting rebellious. I heard the speech at home with my family. My parents and my older sister were crying. All I could think of was what you had said in fourth grade about his nose." Mr. Kimura narrowed his eyes a little, remembering. "By then, your family had moved back to the countryside. I was disappointed to think that I would never run into you again."

"I'm sure you weren't really disappointed."

"Yes, I was. I was very disappointed." Mr. Kimura turned back to Yuki, who had been eating her sandwich as quietly as possible. "Your mother was the brightest student in our class," he said to her. "We all admired her very much."

"That was a long time ago," her mother said. "Now, Mr. Kimura has become a professor. He teaches literature at the Kobe National University."

"But I never forgot your mother. I would have looked her up sooner if I had not been living in Tokyo all this time. I only came back to Kobe this April."

Yuki and her mother had been to Tokyo a few times to visit her aunt Aya. What Yuki remembered most about the city was the way people talked. Her ears hurt from listening to them. They talked fast and loud; they sounded like they enjoyed spitting out their words.

"You don't sound like someone from Tokyo," she said to Mr. Kimura.

"Of course not. I grew up here in Kobe. I never picked up the Tokyo dialect, though I lived there for fifteen years and was married to a woman who spoke the dialect. Even my children speak like Tokyoites."

In Yuki's class, there were a few kids who had moved to Kobe from other parts of the country. They always got teased about their speech. "Do your children get into fights at school because people tease them about how they talk?" she asked Mr. Kimura.

"I don't think so," he said. "Anyway, it's just my son,

and he's already in middle school. My daughter lives in Tokyo with her mother."

"Oh."

"We are divorced."

Yuki considered this for a while. She knew only one girl at school whose parents had been divorced. The girl's name was Mariko; she lived with her father and his parents. Mariko said she scarcely remembered her mother, who had gone to live with her parents in the country. All the same, in May, when their teacher, Mr. Yamasaki, told the class to write essays about their mothers for Mother's Day, Mariko ran out of the room without writing anything. Mr. Yamasaki brought her back and made her sit down. "I don't have a mother," Mariko said. "Write about your grandmother, then," Mr. Yamasaki told her. Mariko sat at her desk all that hour staring at her blank paper and sniffling but did not write a word. When school was over that afternoon, Mr. Yamasaki told Mariko to stay behind while everyone else went home.

Walking home to her mother, Yuki could not stop feeling sorry for Mariko. "Mama," she said as soon as she came into the house, "you wouldn't believe what happened at school today to Mariko. I think Mr. Yamasaki was wrong." Shizuko listened to the story and agreed. "Your teacher shouldn't have been so strict with a poor motherless girl," she said. "Why couldn't Mariko stay with her mother anyway?" Yuki asked then. "Having no father wouldn't be as bad as having no mother." "When a couple gets divorced," Shizuko answered, "the children usually remain with the father while the mother goes back to live with her parents. If there are two or three children, some of them might stay with their mother. But if there's only one child, the mother almost always winds up alone." The way her mother looked at Yuki, her face completely without a smile, Yuki knew what she meant. Like me, she thought but didn't say.

Yuki stared at Mr. Kimura's long, thin face and tried to imagine his daughter. She wondered if his daughter missed him. She couldn't imagine seeing her mother only once a month.

Her mother and Mr. Kimura were talking about a temple they had once visited on a school trip. The temple had a pond with hundreds of carp in it. They were all the colors you could imagine: red, black, white, orange, yellow, peach.

"While we were walking by the pond," Mr. Kimura said to Yuki, "one small carp jumped out of the water and landed on the stone path at our feet. It was the size of our hands and bright yellow, almost golden. It kept flopping around and gasping for breath. Nobody wanted to go near it. We were just watching it die. But your mother stepped up, grabbed the carp by the tail, and threw it back into the water. It swam away. She saved it."

"It was a small thing," her mother said, blushing. Yuki wasn't sure if she meant the carp or her saving it. If what Mr. Kimura had said had been a story, the golden carp would have come back to pay its debt to her mother. In the folktales her mother read to her at night, animals often came back to the people who had rescued them. They brought treasures or granted wishes. Yuki wondered what her mother would have wished for if she had been the heroine of a story like that. Not money or treasure, she was sure. She watched her mother and Mr. Kimura talking and drinking their tea. They were laughing. Her mother had a clear, ringing voice when she laughed.

At nine, Yuki had to go to bed. She said good night and went to get ready while her mother was seeing Mr. Kimura to the door. She could still hear them talking at the gate. She had been lying down a few minutes when she finally heard the sound of his car starting up and pulling away.

That was the night before she had to go to an athletic competition. Every year, the city awarded a prize to the best athlete in each grade. Yuki had been chosen to represent the fourth grade at her school. She was worried about the swimming event. Her breaststroke was all right, and her freestyle had improved since last year. In backstroke, though, she kept weaving all over the lane. She couldn't go straight no matter how hard she tried. Now, the thought of swimming kept her awake. Every time she closed her eyes, she imagined herself drowning or hitting her head on the side. Just when she began to fall asleep, she would wake up flailing her arms and gasping for breath. She kept tossing and turning, almost falling asleep and then being wide awake again. She kicked off the covers and then got cold. But the covers pressed down on her chest so she couldn't breathe. At eleven, she finally gave up and went out of her room in her pajamas.

The kitchen light was on. Her mother usually waited up for her father, to give him his tea. Yuki walked down the hallway toward the light. In the kitchen, her mother was just hanging up the phone. Her face looked pale.

"I couldn't sleep," Yuki said, pulling out a chair and sitting at the table. "Was that Father?" she asked. He often called at the last minute to say that he wasn't coming home.

Her mother didn't answer until she sat down opposite Yuki.

"No, it was Mr. Kimura," she said.

"Oh. Did he forget something?"

Her mother shook her head. "I called him because he had given me his number and said I should call if I needed a friend, someone to talk to."

Yuki noticed the white card in her mother's hand.

"Here," Shizuko said, holding it out to Yuki. "I don't need this anymore."

Yuki took the card. It had Mr. Kimura's name with his business and home addresses and phone numbers printed below it.

Her mother reached across the table and held Yuki's hands. "I'm not going to call Mr. Kimura again," she said.

"Why not? He's your friend."

Her mother shook her head. "I already have a friend if I need someone to talk to." She tilted her head and smiled. "You are my friend, Yuki. I don't have to call anyone else." Though she was smiling, her eyes looked sad.

"But wouldn't Mr. Kimura be waiting for you to call?" Yuki thought of how she hated it when her friends promised to do something and failed to follow through.

"No," her mother said. "I explained everything to him just now. He understands."

They sat in silence for a while. Then her mother said, "You need to sleep for tomorrow. Go back to your room. I'll put the kettle on in case your father comes home soon, and then I'll come and tell you a story so you can sleep."

Yuki went back to her room. She wasn't sure what to do with Mr. Kimura's card. She thought about it for a while and finally put it in her drawer underneath her handkerchiefs. Her mother came and told her a story about a girl who was born from a huge peach and grew up to fight the bad goblins on a far-away island. It was a story everyone knew, but in the original version, the hero was a boy and his followers were a pheasant, a dog, and a monkey. In her mother's telling, she was a girl helped by a cat, a peacock, and a whale who transported them to the island of the goblins. Yuki fell asleep while they were riding the whale back to the girl's house. The next day, she came in second at the competition. Soon, she forgot about Mr. Kimura's card.

Yuki didn't see Mr. Kimura again for three years, until she was living in Tokyo with her aunt Aya. By then, it was the end of February, eleven months after her mother's death. Her father was planning his second wedding. Yuki was scheduled to go back to live with him and his wife as soon as they were married.

One cold evening, while Aya and Yuki were finishing their supper, someone came and knocked on their front door. Aya went to answer. Yuki followed and stood in the hallway, watching.

The man stood in the doorway with his black hat in his hand. "I was a friend of your sister's," he said to Aya. "Your mother gave me your address. I only heard the news two weeks ago, through a friend, so I went to see your mother. She told me your niece is living with you. I wanted to see her. I come to Tokyo once a month to see my daughter." He put his hand on the doorframe and looked down. "If I had known," he said. "If I had only known how truly unhappy she was."

Yuki stepped up from behind her aunt.

Mr. Kimura raised his face. His eyes were red. "Hello," he said to Yuki. "Do you remember me?"

"Yes," Yuki said. "You are my mother's friend from grade school."

Mr. Kimura put his hand on Yuki's shoulder and hugged her. "I'm so sorry to hear about your mother," he said. "I'm so sorry. I know how much she loved you."

Yuki got up from her desk and lay down on her bed, staring at the ceiling. It was completely dark now, but she didn't turn on the light. Downstairs, her father and stepmother were arguing again. Their voices came from their bedroom, directly below her. Soon, a door slammed. Her stepmother must have walked out. Yuki held her breath and listened. The footsteps went down the hallway toward the living room. Another door slammed. Now her stepmother would sit on the couch until her husband came to apologize.

The last time her stepmother shut herself up in the living room like this, a few months ago, her father came up to Yuki's room. He barged in without knocking and said they both should apologize because it was Yuki, more than himself, that her stepmother was angry at.

"It's your stubbornness," he said. "You'll ruin my life with it."

When Yuki hesitated, her father said, "You owe me this. If she leaves me because of you, you'll have to quit school and keep house for me. You're old enough now. Come on. You have no choice."

So she went down with him. Her stepmother talked bitterly about what a selfish person Yuki was, how her mother had spoiled her and taught her nothing.

Yuki turned over onto her stomach and pressed her face into the pillow. Downstairs, her father was walking out of the kitchen. He was going down the hallway. Yuki listened, hoping to hear the living room door click open and then shut behind him. But his footsteps didn't stop. They turned the corner and kept right on up the stairs. He was walking so heavily that the wood rattled under his feet.

Yuki rolled onto her back, ready to get up. Her door had no lock. He would come in any moment and find her lying in the dark. She jumped to her feet and took a step, then stopped, dizzy from standing up too soon. Her vision was full of yellow dots rising and falling. She pressed her fingers to her temples. She was seeing thousands of golden fish jumping up and then splashing back into the water.

If the golden carp had come back to pay its debt, she thought, her mother would have wished for someone to love.

She reached toward the wall and switched on the light. Her father was on the landing. His footsteps stopped. Yuki stood still and tried to compose herself before he swung open the door.

11
Winter Sky
(February 1975)

Because they had both been married once before, the ceremony was short. Her aunt Aya wore a light gray kimono and Mr. Kimura a plain dark suit. They sat in Yuki's grandparents' family room in front of the Buddhist altar. The grandparents, Uncle Saburo and his wife, Etsuko, and Yuki sat in a circle around them. While the priest in his white robe waved a green wand over the couple and chanted, Yuki thought of a story her mother had told her a long time ago. Eight children sat in a circle singing and playing. Sometimes, a ninth child, neither a boy nor a girl, appeared and then disappeared. Soon the other eight noticed and began to chant, "Someone's missing, someone's here, someone's missing, someone's here," while the ninth child continued to appear and disappear. The chant whirled around Yuki's mind the way the bare trees of February had flown past the train window early that morning on her way. For the second time after her mother's death and her father's remarriage, Yuki saw the rice paddies and the rivers of the countryside she had visited every summer with her mother. The scenery looked unfamiliar in winter. Coming home, she thought, all the same; I am coming home to my mother's family.

The priest left shortly after the ceremony. Yuki went to the kitchen to help Etsuko prepare the food. It was to be a simple traditional celebration dinner: rice with red azuki beans, greens, a red sea bream. Etsuko was already cleaning the fish at the counter. She was expecting in less than a month. She stood back from the counter a little to leave room for her stomach and to let her shoulders lean forward over the cutting board. The knife in her right hand made swishing sounds as she scaled the fish.

"I should do that," Yuki said, standing behind her, uncertain. She didn't think she could do it.

"Oh, no, I like preparing fish." Etsuko didn't look back. After she finished scaling the fish, she cut a long, straight opening in its stomach and took out dark red parts. Yuki looked away. The fish would be baked whole. Its skin would be slightly wrinkled but glistening, tinted orange, and underneath, the flesh would be packed like fallen peony petals, pinkish white. Yuki wouldn't be able to eat the fish, and Uncle Saburo would make fun of her the way he had made fun of her squeamishness all her life, those times he had gone fishing for bass or pike and she had refused to eat any of them. She hadn't seen Saburo since the third anniversary of her mother's death; she had never met Etsuko till this morning. Still, she knew that they would tease her. She wasn't sure whether the thought amused or irritated her. She had always been particular about what she could and could not eat. Her stepmother often cooked things she could not eat, pink shrimp with their tiny legs and feelers curled around themselves, little clams in their shells, boiled quail eggs smaller than her thumbnail. Sick to her stomach, Yuki would sit at the table sipping her glass of water. Her stepmother would say nothing. As soon as Yuki got up from the table, her stepmother would reach out for the plate and scrape the untouched food into the wastebasket, glaring at Yuki but still saying nothing.

"I'll manage the fish," Etsuko said. "You can wash the greens and the rice."

Standing at the sink, Yuki washed first the rice and then the greens. The greens consisted of Chinese cabbage and the leaves and tiny buds of *kikuna*, edible spring mums. They reminded her of the daisies and nasturtiums her mother had put into salads, straight from her garden, fragrant and bittersweet. They tasted the way Yuki had always imagined light to taste. She left the greens drying in the colander and went to the cupboards to take out the plates and bowls they would need to set the table.

She knew exactly where everything was kept—her grandmother's good white china with designs in relief of tiny petals, the red-lacquered chopsticks. It was the same as when she was a child; she would come home to her mother's family every summer and find everything in the same place, year after year. Her grandparents' house seemed more familiar now than her father's, where her stepmother had replaced everything. Sunday mornings before track meets, Yuki went downstairs for orange juice and still missed her mother's white ceramic goblets, how the orange juice looked like the full moon in them. Now, she had only the pictures in her sketchbook. When the new, fragile glasses and plates broke or chipped, her stepmother just went to a department store and bought more. There seemed to be no end of glasses and plates that looked exactly the same.

Yuki put the china on a tray and walked to the family room. There, they would set up the black-lacquered table and sit on the floor in front of the altar to eat their festive dinner.

As she entered the room, Yuki saw that her uncle had already set up the table and everybody was sitting on the floor, drinking the tea Etsuko had brought earlier. Aya and Mr. Kimura sat side by side. Her grandmother, her grandfather, and her uncle Saburo each took one side of the table. In the last three years, her grandmother had grown thinner while her grandfather had become stout. Her grandmother still sounded pretty much the same. She talked fast in her high-pitched voice. Her grandfather, though, sometimes paused in the middle of his sentences now, to collect his thoughts or his breath, Yuki could not tell which. As soon as she had walked into the house, she had noticed the change in him. Everything about him had slowed down. Because his legs had gotten weak, he now had to walk with a cane. Each step seemed to take a deliberate effort. His face turned red and he breathed heavily. During the short wedding ceremony, Yuki had sat directly opposite him. In the light from the window, his eyes looked wet, and he kept blinking. Yuki wasn't sure if he was crying or if the light was hurting his eyes. Her grandfather didn't cry easily. He hadn't even cried at his daughter's funeral. He said that Shizuko was at peace, going to join the spirits of their ancestors; that they should be thankful. Yuki had known how sad he really was, but only from the way his voice had cracked from time to time.

Yuki knelt down next to her grandmother, set the tray on the tatami floor, and began to distribute the plates and bowls. She set seven places, putting Etsuko next to

Saburo and herself next to her grandmother. Everyone, except her grandfather, continued to talk about Mr. Kimura's job at the national university in Kobe. Her grandfather was silently watching Yuki.

"We should set another place, shouldn't we?" he said abruptly. "For your mother."

Yuki's grandmother turned away from the conversation. All talk seemed to stop. Yuki put the last plate on the table and then the chopsticks.

"What a strange thing to say," her grandmother said. She forced a short laugh. "We would bring bad luck to the wedding. We don't want that."

Her grandfather said nothing. Mr. Kimura resumed the conversation. Yuki lifted the lid of the teapot. It was only half empty. Still, she took it and stood up to go back to the kitchen.

"Leave the teapot and sit with us now," Saburo said.

Everybody nodded toward Yuki. She sat down next to her grandmother.

"Mr. Kimura has been telling us about the national university," Saburo continued. "It's a shame that you are not going there in April."

"It's too late to think about that," Yuki said. "The exams are already over." She had told them that after her graduation from high school in March, she planned to go to a small college in Nagasaki to study art.

"But you have good grades," Aya said. She looked toward Mr. Kimura and then back to Yuki. "He thinks he can arrange a special exam for you in the next week. If you do well, you can still get in. Some people always decide to go somewhere else at the last minute. You can take their place."

Mr. Kimura also turned to Yuki. "I'm sure you'll do

well on the exam. You don't have to think I did a favor for you. You would be doing us a favor by coming to our school."

"Thank you," Yuki said, addressing just Mr. Kimura. "But my mind is already made up. I am going to Nagasaki. I have been planning it for a long time."

"Why Nagasaki?" her grandmother asked. "It's so far away, clear on another island. We'll never be able to see you. Besides, your uncle's school has a better reputation."

"I couldn't care less about reputation," Yuki said to her grandmother. "The school I'm going to is a good school for art. I would be happier there. National universities are for people who are ambitious, who want to work for big companies in the future. That isn't for me. My teachers agreed. I wouldn't fit in at a national university. I don't want to fit in."

Her grandmother frowned at her. Her eyes had gotten to be a paler brown than they used to be. They looked oddly defenseless.

"You have to understand," Yuki continued, trying to be patient. "I need to go to a school far away. I couldn't go to the national university or any other school in Kobe because my father and his wife wouldn't let me move out of their house then. They would worry about what people would say; people would think it strange for me to be moving away from home to go to a school only twenty minutes away by train. If I go to Nagasaki, though, my parents can say that I have gone to a special school on another island. They don't have to lose face about my moving out."

"You have talked about this with them?" Saburo asked.

"No," Yuki said, off her guard. Everyone stared at her. There was nothing to do but tell the truth. "Actually, I haven't talked about any of my plans with them. But I know what they think. I mentioned going to Nagasaki once to my stepmother, about a month ago, but I don't know if she was listening. She was cutting up something for my father's lunch. She didn't even look in my direction when I spoke. She and I seldom talk to each other anyway, except when she's very upset with me. Then she talks a lot and I have to listen." Yuki took a deep breath.

Nobody spoke for a while. Saburo was picking up and putting down his chopsticks. Her grandmother poured herself another cup of tea. Aya and Mr. Kimura sat perfectly still, and her grandfather seemed to be staring at the plates. Back in the kitchen, Etsuko was cutting up the greens. Yuki heard the staccato pounding of the knife.

"What does it matter to you?" Yuki said, "or to me? In a month, I'll be gone to Nagasaki and I'll never hear from them or write to them. I'm not going to take any money from them. I've been saving from my job at the library. I worked every night so I wouldn't have to ask them for any money to go to college. And so long as I'm not living with them, I can start coming here every summer just like before." Yes, she thought, then it would be as though the last six years had never happened.

"But they are your parents," her grandmother said. She picked up her cup and brought it down without drinking from it. "You have to show them some respect. I'm glad you want to see us, but still, we can't encourage you to neglect your duty by them. It wouldn't be right."

"How can I respect them?" Yuki asked. "They show no respect for me or for my mother, or for you. They were married only a year after her death. They knew each other while she was alive. You might even say they were waiting for her to die."

"You don't know what was between them in the past," Saburo said. "You shouldn't jump to conclusions. Just because they worked in the same office, it doesn't mean anything."

"But I know. I live with them. I can tell. How I treat them is really none of your business anyway."

Her grandmother opened her mouth as if to say something and then stopped. She brought her hand to her face and covered her mouth. Her thin shoulders heaved up and down. She shook her head slowly.

Yuki put her hands on her grandmother's shoulders. "I'm sorry," she said. "Please don't be upset."

Her grandmother turned away, stiffening her shoulders.

"Sometimes," her grandfather said suddenly, "you have to show respect to other people before you can expect it from them."

Startled, Yuki looked toward him. He had not even turned to her to speak. He was still staring at the table. She could not tell whether his comment was meant as a rebuke or just a remark, or whether he knew what he was saying. They are the adults, I shouldn't have to teach them about respect, she wanted to say, but she stopped herself. Her grandfather grabbed his cane and was trying to stand up. He leaned on his right arm a few times and then gave up. Instead, he let go of the cane and started moving on his hands and knees around the low table toward Yuki and her grandmother. Yuki noticed how his cheeks, red from effort, had gotten more wrinkled and pouchy in the last three years. From the kitchen, she could smell the baking fish, the salty smell of the sea and the burning flesh. She stood up. Her grandfather stopped, his shoulders moving with his breathing. Uncle Saburo put his hand on his father's back, as if to support him or to hold him back. Her grandfather's face was gray and sad. Yuki could scarcely look at him.

"I need fresh air," she said. "I'm going outside for a while. I didn't mean to offend anybody. I'm so sorry."

She started walking, walking faster, running. She went through the front door, ran across the yard to the back of the house, and then to the persimmon tree farthest away from the house.

She was cold without her jacket. Shivering, she leaned back against the trunk and closed her eyes. She thought of the priest's wand waving over Aya and Mr. Kimura, her father and her stepmother, her father and her mother a long time ago, Aya and her first husband, and even before that, Mr. Kimura and his first wife. Each time the wand moved exactly the same way while a priest in a white robe chanted the same words. Her grandparents, too, were married in the same ceremony more than fifty years ago. She thought of them now, her grandmother turning away from her angrily, her grandfather too weak to rise to his feet and walk. Ten years ago, her grandfather used to outwalk her on a mountain path. His black hiking shoes came down heavily and steadily. Often, he got ahead of her. He would wait for her, and together, they would run down the last hill. At the bottom, her mother would stand holding white peonies she was bringing to the family graves. Yuki's thoughts wandered to Etsuko, her stomach big with child, splitting the fish's stomach and taking out the red entrails. Still shivering, Yuki opened her eyes and looked up. The bare branches of the persimmon tree looked like a net spread under the steely blue sky of a late-winter afternoon. Between the house and the tree, where her grandmother's flowers would be in the spring, the plots were frozen hard. The bench that was placed under the persimmon tree in the summer was gone for the winter, stored in the shed with all the tools useless now till spring.

When Yuki was a child, her grandfather had sat on the bench with her in the evenings and shown her the summer constellations. He had connected the stars, shiny dots, into people and animals, into stories. The tree was full of soft green leaves then. In the fall, the leaves turned pinkish orange and fell. After that, the tree would bear bright red bell-shaped fruit on the otherwise empty branches. Yuki knew this only from the pictures her uncle had sent her. By the time the tree bore fruit, she was back in Kobe, back to school. The fruit was bitter when it came off the tree. But her grandfather would stand on a ladder and pick all the ripe ones, then dry them on long skewers hung on the wall. When they were dried, the persimmons turned very sweet. Every December, her grandfather sent a large box of dried persimmons to the city, and Yuki and her mother would eat them through the winter, reminders of their summer in the country. All that, Yuki thought, was a long time ago. Her mother had been gone for six years. Her grandmother now wanted her to show respect to her father. How can she say such a thing? she wondered. She knows how badly he treated my mother, her own daughter. Yuki sighed and looked toward the house. Mr. Kimura was coming through the back door, holding something in his arms. She watched him as he made his way toward the persimmon tree.

When he was close, she saw he was holding her jacket, the sea green one she had saved money to buy the winter before. She had spent the whole afternoon in downtown Kobe trying to buy just the jacket her mother might have bought her.

Mr. Kimura stood next to Yuki and handed her the jacket. "You must be cold," he said.

She put on the jacket and buttoned it up. Mr. Kimura was looking up at the bare branches.

"I'm sorry about what I said in the house," Yuki said. "I didn't mean to be rude. Maybe I shouldn't have come."

"The last time I saw your mother," he said, "we went to see the pine tree that you said looked like a fox in a wedding dress. But when we stood right in front of the tree, by the breakwater, the tree didn't look much like anything. I guess the distance was wrong. You needed to be farther away to see. That was before I drove her home and the three of us had tea in your kitchen."

The image of the tree floated into Yuki's mind, green in the middle of winter, framed in the center of the kitchen window. It would still be there, by the sea. She wondered if the people who lived in the house now had noticed it.

"I thought about that again last night. Your mother called me later that night and said it was the last time she would call or see me. She said she was too unhappy to be my friend, it wouldn't be right. I tried to persuade her to let me see her now and then, just as a friend, but she wouldn't change her mind."

"I know she called you," Yuki said.

"Do you? I suppose she told you. You were very close to her."

"Yes. She couldn't be your friend because of me."

Mr. Kimura nodded. "I wanted you to be at my wedding because I wouldn't have met Aya if it wasn't for you. Your bringing us together was the one good thing that came out of so much sadness. I'm glad you came."

Yuki surveyed the frozen garden before her. There was something she wanted to ask him. On the train that morning, she had thought of many different ways to ask it. But there was no tactful way, she realized. She turned to Mr. Kimura.

"Did you marry Aunt Aya because she reminded you of my mother?" she asked.

Mr. Kimura looked her straight in the eyes the way very few adults did. "Yes," he said. "Do you think that's bad?"

"I don't know," she said.

"It doesn't mean that I don't love Aya for herself. I think that we often love someone because at least initially, that person reminds us of someone else, someone we have loved before. I don't think there's anything wrong with it."

"I wouldn't know. I don't think I've ever loved anyone except my mother and my grandparents and Aunt Aya and people like that—my mother's family."

"But there must have been boys you have at least liked," he said. He wasn't smiling. He wasn't teasing her. He was serious.

Yuki thought about the boys at school. In her mind,

she always pictured them huddled together, tittering about something—the way some girl's slip showed under the hem of her skirt, the tight blouse of a fat girl, an awkward tall girl's slouch. The ones who didn't huddle and titter, the smart ones, the popular ones, hung around in twos and threes, and often went about with tall girls who also came in twos and threes. These girls wore slim dresses to school. When they passed by, Yuki could smell the faint fragrance of their face powder. During lunch, while the unpopular boys huddled in the hallways and the popular boys and girls walked about the school ground and the other girls sat in the cafeteria, Yuki went out to the track and ran laps. One fast, one slow, one fast, one slow, until her legs, shoulders, and arms hurt. She would shower quickly and go to her fifth-hour class, and after all the afternoon classes, she would change into her gym clothes again and go to cross-country or track practice, depending on which season it was. By the time she had to go home to eat dinner with her father and his wife, she was usually so tired that she could hear a humming in her ear. She would sit quietly and focus on the dull pain in her legs and shoulders, concentrate on those concrete pains. Then she would go to work at the library, shelving or labeling books or writing up order forms. She came home at eleven at night to do her homework. There was no time to sit around and daydream about boys. The only person she had daydreamed about was Sachiko, three years ago. After their summer of running together, Yuki saw her only a few times, when Sachiko came to watch track meets to cheer for her former teammates. By then, Sachiko had stopped running. She congratulated Yuki for winning and then went to join her friends. Now, Sachiko had gone to college. Even before that, Yuki could tell that she, too, was turning into a girl with makeup who walked about with boys.

"No," she said to Mr. Kimura. "I don't think I've ever liked any boy. Do you think that's odd?"

"Not at all. Maybe you'll like somebody later on. I don't think there's any hurry about something like that."

"No, there isn't," she said. "I don't think I'll ever want to be in love. Half the time it doesn't turn out right."

He didn't seem offended or even surprised. He continued to look into her face.

"Of course I don't mean that about you and Aunt Aya," Yuki added. "I was thinking more about my father and my mother. They loved each other once."

"Yes," he said. "And I was married once myself. We got divorced, as you know."

"And Aunt Aya. When she first married, she must have loved her husband. It never occurred to her that in only three years, he would die in a traffic accident. The other people weren't seriously hurt. He died on the spot from hitting his head. She could never foresee that. He didn't even drive that much." Yuki thought for a second and then went on. "I believe that if we could foresee the future, none of us would ever fall in love. It comes to nothing one way or the other."

Mr. Kimura leaned back against the tree, his arms folded. He seemed to be thinking for a long time. Finally, he said, "When I was younger and my marriage was going badly, I used to think the same thing too. What's the point? It all turns out badly. I felt that way again when I heard about your mother's death. I was forty then. But in the last few years, as I've gotten to be forty-five and forty-six, I began to think differently. I think now that it's worth it all the same, loving someone. It may not turn out right, but I want to love someone in spite of it. In a way it means more because the odds are against us. If I didn't think that, I would never have married Aya."

Yuki tried to imagine it—herself at forty-five feeling that love was worthwhile. It was difficult. All she could think of was herself now running around the track, a fast lap, a slow lap, endlessly, while the others fell in love.

The distant sound of the door interrupted her thoughts. She looked toward the house. Aya was coming through the back door in her light gray kimono, a white knit shawl over her shoulders. She was walking toward them in the slow, steady way women in kimonos walked. Mr. Kimura had noticed her; his body was turned toward her, slightly leaning in her direction even though she was still quite far away. Yuki thought of Aya's first wedding. She had only been four, so she remembered little except that at the reception dinner, they had served carrots cut like flowers. And there were yellow chrysanthemums on the tables and her mother was wearing a light blue kimono hand-embroidered with flowers and leaves in a darker blue.

Aya was only about ten steps away now. She smiled at Mr. Kimura, and he began to walk toward her. Yuki realized that it didn't matter what she had said to her grandparents—Aya and Mr. Kimura were too happy now to be offended. They stood together. He was straightening out her white shawl, which had slipped off one of her shoulders.

Yuki looked away from them at the webwork of

branches above her, the sky so far behind them like an endless pit she could fall into backward. She tried to imagine the persimmons in the fall, bright orange bells on bare branches, promises of untasted sweetness. But she had never seen them, except in photographs. She closed her eyes. In a moment, she would walk back to the house, to take her mother's place as best she could among her family. Opening her eyes slowly, she wished for her mother, her grandfather of ten years ago, someone, to read the sky at night, to name the winter stars.

12
Gladioli
(March 1975)

The attic was dark and cold. Yuki climbed through the trapdoor and shone her flashlight at the walls lined with cardboard boxes. Moving the light across the room, she found the three wooden boxes on the floor, exactly where she and her aunt Aya had left them. Yuki had half expected to see the attic empty. She pulled the cord that hung from the ceiling and blinked under the sudden yellow light.

It was past midnight. She had waited until her father and stepmother were sleeping. Careful not to make any noise, she walked slowly toward the wooden boxes and knelt on the floor next to them.

Yuki was to leave for Nagasaki in two days. Having paid her tuition and a month's rent at the rooming house she found through the paper, she had barely enough money for the train ticket. She couldn't afford to send any of her mother's things, but she could pack a small bag to take with her on the train. She was sure that her stepmother would throw out whatever she didn't take. It was a wonder she had not gotten to the attic already.

Yuki opened the box closest to her and found clothes stacked to the top. The first one she took out was a dark purple kimono with hand-dyed patterns of maple leaves and cranes. Yuki put it in her lap and traced the patterns with her fingertips. Her mother had worn kimonos only on very formal occasions. The last time Yuki saw her wear this kimono was the afternoon she went to a neighbor's wedding, when Yuki was eleven. If her mother had lived, she might have worn it to Yuki's graduation from high school, a week ago. Yuki laid the kimono on top of the box lid, which she had set aside. The floor was dusty. She couldn't put anything there.

Next, she took out a teal-blue dress and laid it on top of the kimono. Reaching back into the box, she brought out more dresses, skirts, blouses. When the box lid was full, she opened the other two boxes and used their lids. The smell of mothballs rose from the layers of clothing, but even when she got to the bottom, there were no mothballs. They had evaporated, leaving only the essence of their pungency among the clothes. At the bottom, there were several small boxes, each containing a piece of jewelry: the abalone pin Yuki had given her on Mother's Day, the pearl necklace her mother had bought when they went to see the pearl divers in a small village northeast of Kobe, the coral earrings her father had given her before they were married. Yuki placed the jewelry on top of the clothes.

Each piece that she unpacked was familiar. She remembered her mother wearing it, and she remembered Aya putting it into the box. When she closed her eyes, she could see her mother smiling at her in her teal-blue dress or white linen suit, and at the same time, she could hear the rustle of cottons and silks as Aya folded the clothes and, downstairs, the undertaker's men moving the furniture in the living room.

Yuki opened her eyes and looked at the piles. In the

other boxes, there would be sweaters and coats, more jewelry, shawls, scarves, books, photographs.

Even before she knew exactly what she had decided to do, Yuki started putting the jewelry and the clothes back into the box. Now and then, she pressed a blouse to her cheek, ran her fingers along the lapels of jackets, looked long at the embroidery and the buttons on the dresses. When she was done, she closed all three boxes and sat thinking.

She remembered the afternoon she got up to give a three-minute speech in her sophomore class on Monet's *Gladioli*, a painting she loved. Standing at the podium, she smiled at her classmates and the teacher. She was never nervous about speaking in public. She glanced at the few notes she had jotted down. *Camille's parasol*, the first note read. That was the detail she was going to mention first because she thought it was the most striking thing about the painting—a woman, Monet's wife, holding a green parasol in the upper-left corner. But when she looked back at the class to start speaking, she was suddenly struck dumb. Why should I mention the parasol more than the flowers or the sky or the brush-strokes or the colors? she wondered. The next moment, she realized that she couldn't talk about the painting in three minutes; if she had three hours or three days, she still couldn't do it. Whatever was important about the painting simply could not be put into a speech. This thought made her heart beat faster, but not from ner-vousness or distress. She felt tremendously happy. She stood for her three minutes without saying anything, smiled, bowed, and sat down. The only true thing she could say on that occasion, she thought even now, was nothing. She had sat down after her silent speech feeling as though she was filled with the bright blue and green brushstrokes on Monet's canvas.

Yuki put her hand on the box she had unpacked and then packed again. Her mother couldn't be summed up in a list any more than Monet's painting could be described in a three-minute speech. It would be wrong to take any ten or twenty things as though her mother had been nothing but an assortment of dresses, necklaces, and a few photographs; as though one dress represented her more than the others, one piece of jewelry over another. Yuki was sure now. To save a few things and leave the others was to say that her mother could be reduced to one essence, like the mothballs that disappeared in every way except their smell. She would not do that.

Yuki took her flashlight, stood up, and turned off the ceiling light. In the dark, her flashlight shone against the boxes along the wall. She went to one of them and touched the white label. Her mother's neat handwriting was still clear: *Yuki's Watercolors, Fifth and Sixth Grades*. Every box along the wall contained something from her childhood. She and her mother had packed them a long time ago. "We'll look at these things together when we're both old," her mother had said. "We'll remember your childhood and talk." They would never be old together.

It's all right, Yuki told herself in spite of the terrible sadness she still felt. These things were not necessary for her to go on remembering. In her sketchbook, she had drawn pictures of the clothes her mother had made for her, and of the pottery they had bought and used together. Even more than that, she had the memory in her mind. Though she and her mother would never be old together, Yuki would still remember her and their time together when she was an old woman.

Through the trapdoor, Yuki climbed down into the closet of the room that used to be her mother's. As she stepped out of the closet, she pointed her flashlight across the floor. There was nothing except piles of magazines and newspapers her stepmother had put against one wall. The room had been unused for years. Soon, her own room would look the same. Her stepmother would throw out her desk and bed, even her quilted futon and the books she was leaving behind.

Walking quietly across the stairway landing, Yuki went back to her room, changed into her pajamas in the dark, and lay down on the bed. She tried to imagine the countryside outside the train window on her way to Nagasaki. The rice paddies would already be flooded. They would be squares of warm muddy brown—blank spaces waiting to be filled with green seedlings in another month.

My mother and I, Yuki thought, we are moving on. We leave behind nothing but empty spaces—empty spaces turning green as we move away from here.

13
Silent Spring
(March 1975)

A week after his daughter, Yuki, left for a college in Nagasaki, Hideki came home from work and found cardboard boxes stacked up outside his door. There were eight of them, arranged in neat double rows as if left ready for a delivery truck. He hurried into the house and went straight to the kitchen, where his wife, Hanae, would be preparing supper.

"Why did you put those boxes outside the door?" he asked as he stood in the doorway.

Hanae was chopping some vegetables at the sink. Hideki walked in and stood behind her. The sink was scattered with peelings of potatoes, chopped-off tops and tails of carrots, onion skins. Hanae stopped her hand for a minute and looked up; she did not turn around to face him.

"Yuki didn't take them, so I thought I was justified in throwing them out. The attic's been so cluttered." She went back to chopping the carrots.

"But what are they?" Hideki asked. At any rate, he knew, they were not Hanae's own things. "Yuki's things that she didn't take?"

Hanae stopped chopping again. "They are the things that had been stored in the boxes in the attic before I came," she said. "Clothes, mostly. Then there are boxes of Yuki's old things that had been packed up and saved. There's plenty more of that junk in the attic for another day."

Hideki remained silent. Hanae would never mention his first wife, Shizuko, by name, but every time she was mentioned indirectly, there was an awkwardness.

"Yuki would have taken them if she wanted them," Hanae said.

"I'm not so sure." Hideki looked around for a place to put down his briefcase but there was nowhere except for the tabletop, which would have to be cleared soon. He kept the briefcase. "Maybe she didn't take those things because she has no space for them where she's living. From the address, it sounded like a lodging, a one-room place. She probably doesn't get to store anything there. Besides, she must not have had much money to send things by mail. I imagine she had just enough to pay the first installment of the tuition and get through the first month. She must have had to save everything she could. I don't know, but she may very well want the things later."

Hanae abruptly turned away from the sink and glared at him. "You anger me," she said, "the way you were with her. You had absolutely no authority over her. How could you let her go without knowing exactly where and how she was going to live? I don't care about her. A selfish girl like that, she'll manage all right for herself. But you know what the neighbors are thinking even this moment. They're thinking that I drove her away from her own house because I was a bad stepmother. Anyone can tell she left all of a sudden, without telling us much. They'll see how she never comes back even for short visits. They'll say it was all my fault."

Hanae stood very rigid. Her angry breathing was audible. Hideki put the briefcase down on the floor and reached toward her, to put his hand on her shoulder, but she pulled back. He stared for a moment at his outstretched hand and then drew it back. Hanae forced a laugh.

"From the way she left," she said, "you know she'll never write to us or ask us for anything. I wouldn't be surprised if you never heard from her, except to say in four years that she's graduating and moving somewhere else, or that she's getting married, if she ever does."

Hideki thought again about the morning Yuki had left. She came down to the kitchen while they were having their breakfast. Standing in the doorway with a suitcase in her hand, she said, "I'll leave the address of my lodging by the telephone, just in case you need to get in touch with me someday. But you don't have to write unless there's something important. I don't think I will, either." Hideki had been unable to say anything. Hanae had put down her chopsticks and stared at Yuki, her jaw set so hard he could almost feel the tension in her teeth. Yuki's face looked pale. "I'm calling a cab to the train station now," she said. "I don't think I'll ever come back here." Then she turned around and walked out. From the hallway Hideki could hear her dialing the cab and giving the address. Soon, there was the sound of the door closing. That was all. She was gone.

Hanae had gone back to her chopping. Over its staccato noise, she said, "I was going to ask you to burn those boxes. The garbage pickup isn't until early next week. If we leave them outside, the neighbors' children

151

might pull things out, and then their parents might talk. You know how it is." Her voice was no longer angry, but casual, almost conciliatory.

Hideki rolled his head back and stared at the white ceiling. Then, to loosen the tight knot in the back of his neck, he slowly rolled his head from right to left and listened to his neck cracking. All week, he had been trying to remember exactly how he had felt at Yuki's leaving. He could hardly deny it. He had felt a surge of relief and, immediately thereafter, a sense of annoyance and guilt—guilt, he thought now as he listened to the cracking of his neck, about being glad to have her gone. Beyond that, he had felt very little. With Yuki gone, there would be no more arguments with Hanae unless he himself were to anger her.

"When do you want me to burn the boxes?" he asked her. "Right now?"

"Oh, you don't have to rush around like that." Hanae stopped chopping and took the empty kettle off the stove. She turned the faucet and filled the kettle. "Supper's going to be ready in an hour or so. I'll put the kettle on right now so you can have some tea while you wait. Why don't you sit down? You should relax after a hard day's work. You can burn the boxes after supper if you feel up to it." She turned sideways toward him, smiling, as she placed the kettle on the stove. "Yes, that would be very helpful," she said, "if you could burn them after supper."

The fire was just beginning to catch. Hideki squatted in the backyard after sundown beside the boxes, watching the small flames around the crumpled balls of newspaper he used as kindling. It was slow going. The ground was still damp from the rain of the night before. It had been another wet March, but even the evening air was warmer now, almost balmy. One more week, Hideki thought, and it would be April. Schools—Yuki's college too—would start a new year then. Hideki continued to watch the fire, keeping count of the time in his mind. High school graduation had been in mid-March. Yuki had not asked him or his wife, and they had not gone. Hanae was annoyed: people would talk, she said, about how Yuki's parents didn't even care to attend her graduation; they would say that it was because Yuki had only a stepmother, not a real mother. She had expected him to intervene, to make Yuki invite them, but he didn't try because he knew Yuki would simply refuse. "No," she might say, "I don't invite people I don't like." That was the kind of thing she said on the few occasions when she talked to them. She was blunt and stubborn. She talked as though he was a stranger, not her father at all but a stranger she didn't like. Perhaps that was how she thought of him. There was no denying, Hideki thought now, that the situation at home had been as intolerable to Yuki as it was to Hanae. She had left as soon as she possibly could—giving herself just a week after graduation to quit her part-time job at the city library, pack up, send some of the things, perhaps. Hideki did not know exactly what she had done or thought in that week. He wondered if she had wanted the things he was about to burn. She might have left them on purpose because she wanted to forget all of her past. Or perhaps it had been too painful for her to go through her mother's things even now. That was most likely. It had been six years since Shizuko's death, but he had to admit that Yuki had never gotten over it.

The fire began to smolder. He would have to feed it

slowly, taking the things out of the boxes and casting them in a little at a time. Inside the first box he opened, he found large envelopes and manila folders of paper and photographs. These must be the things Shizuko had saved from Yuki's childhood. They would burn easily. After he tossed them into the fire by large handfuls, he pulled open the other boxes and emptied the two that contained more folders. The flames rose higher.

Long ago when he was a child, the people in his town celebrated the last day of each year by building a bonfire in the field behind the town hall. Each family brought a year's worth of newspapers, letters, bills, old clothes, anything they wanted to get rid of. The fire burned all night. Monks from nearby temples came to beat drums and chant. The bonfire was a ritual of cleansing, of putting things behind and moving on into the new year. Of all the old-fashioned rituals, Hideki thought now, that fire was the best. It taught people to put things behind, forget, embrace the new.

By the time he got to the clothes, his fire was burning steadily. He reached inside the first box of clothes and pulled things out without looking. As he dropped them in, they felt cool and slippery. A few of them caught fire immediately and kindled while the others burned slowly.

Someone should have taught Yuki to forget the past, Hideki thought as he squatted to watch the fire. Each time Hanae had threatened to leave him, it was Yuki's fault. Yuki should have tried harder to forget her mother and love Hanae. Instead, she had stayed away from home as much as possible and spent all her time in her room when she had to be home. She came down only at mealtimes, and then spoke not a word at the table.

Sometimes, she didn't even eat. She sat drinking her glass of water and got up to leave as soon as it was polite to do so. "Your daughter acts like we don't even exist," Hanae had complained. "She has nothing but contempt for us, and she won't even hide it." Hanae was angry with him because he could not make Yuki behave differently. She said it was all his fault. He had allowed her to be brought up as a spoiled, selfish girl.

Hideki distinctly remembered the first time Hanae had threatened to leave, about a year after their marriage. In the middle of supper one evening, without much of a warning, Hanae got up from the table saying, "You make me sick, the two of you, sick. You're close and sly, Yuki. All the time, you're silent, not a word, but who knows what you're plotting in your head, and you"—she glared at Hideki—"you are totally useless. If she were my daughter, she'd be taught to behave differently." Hanae left the kitchen, and for a while, Hideki remained seated, thinking that she had gone to wash her face, to compose herself, until he heard the front door slam. Then he had to find his shoes, his jacket, and run after her. When he caught up with her about three blocks away from the house, she was standing on the street trying to hail a cab, clutching her purse tight against her chest. She did not resist being brought back. They walked slowly home, without speaking. Yuki had already gone up to her room. Hanae went into the living room and sat on the couch for two hours in silence, while Hideki apologized and pleaded with her not to leave him. Just before they went to bed that night, he saw her take a pair of underwear out of her purse and put it back in her drawer. He realized then that was all she had packed in her purse before running away.

Hideki stood up to throw more things into the fire. In the unsteady light, he could not clearly make out the clothes he must have seen once. He tried to picture the way Shizuko used to dress. I must still remember at least one dress, one coat, one piece of jewelry, he thought. But nothing came to his mind. She had, it seemed to him, preferred blues and greens, colors of the water. But he was not completely sure. After the first few years, he had spent little time at home. Even now, he wondered if they should have been divorced, if that might have saved her. But divorce would have been disgraceful and impractical. Yuki had been born by then. She would have been left with him since she was his only child. Then there would have been the same problems between Yuki and his second wife, Yuki and himself. Hideki could not remember a time when he had felt a strong bond with Yuki. Even before her mother's death, she was a strange, quiet child to him, though other people said she was cheerful and likable. Most of the time, he wanted to have nothing to do with her. The thought of Yuki, as far as he could remember, brought him nothing but a useless sense of guilt—guilt for her mother's unhappiness, guilt for her eventual suicide, for which, Hideki knew, Yuki held him responsible. After that, there was guilt for his remarriage, for keeping her away from her mother's family according to Hanae's wishes because Hanae thought people would talk—they would see the continued contact between Yuki and his former in-laws as an admission of blame on his part for his first wife's death. Guilt was a useless emotion, Hideki reminded himself. Still, the list of his wrongs seemed endless. Now he was burning what was Yuki's legacy—her mother's clothes, the things her mother had saved for her.

But I have no other way, Hideki thought. I have to live in peace with Hanae. Everybody knew that his first wife had committed suicide. He could not add to that disgrace by having his second wife run away. It had taken much courage, he reminded himself as he watched the flames and the smoke, to go on at the company after Shizuko's death instead of resigning as some people had expected him to do. This time, if Hanae were to leave him, there would be no choice. People would no longer give him the benefit of the doubt. They would no longer assume that he had been unlucky in his first marriage, that he had married an unstable woman who would have killed herself no matter who her husband was. If Hanae were to leave, he would be expected to step down from his supervisory position. A man who had had two wives and could not control either of them was not fit to supervise other men. But that wasn't the only important thing, Hideki told himself: Hanae did love him. She had loved him, she once said, since the first day she came to work as a secretary at his office. That was more than fifteen years ago. Hanae had been just twenty-two, a mere girl, who then continued to love him for nine, ten years before he was widowed and could marry her. There was much to be said, Hideki thought, for such love and loyalty.

As he pulled open the last box and put his hand inside, his fingers touched something hard. He pulled it out and squinted in the glow of the fire. It was a large notebook; its sturdy blue cardboard cover seemed familiar. Stepping back a few paces from the fire, he continued to stare at the notebook. It was Shizuko's sketchbook. He remembered it from the days before their marriage when he was hospitalized with tuberculosis and she used to sit by his bed making watercolor sketches while they talked. His face felt hot from the fire. He was beginning to sweat. He got up, emptied the rest of the box into the fire, stepped back, and crouched again. With the unopened sketchbook still in his hand, he found himself thinking of Shizuko's face—in death, her face was almost peaceful, as though she had completely forgotten him. She did not even leave a note for him—just one for Yuki, which she would not show him. Nothing for him. Silence. Sweating still, Hideki looked up at the balmy early-spring sky.

Three years ago on a warm spring evening like this, Yuki's grandmother had called him and asked him to let Yuki visit them, to attend the third anniversary of Shizuko's death. Hideki had given in because the old woman's voice sounded broken down and pathetic, and he couldn't bear to listen to her any longer. "Fine, I'll send her," he had said, and hung up. That was the only time he had gone against Hanae's wishes. He had given his consent over the phone; when his wife found out and got angry, it was too late. He had also tried to save some pottery that she was going to throw out. It was a tea set, he remembered. But he had never told Yuki that he had saved it for her, afraid she would blame him then for not having saved anything else. In the end, the pottery seemed to have been thrown out anyway. He never confronted Hanae about it. Hideki gripped the sketchbook and looked at the fire, considering. He thought of the address Yuki had written down on a piece of paper by the telephone. He could almost see her small, cramped-up handwriting. All right, he thought. I will save the sketchbook and send it. Hanae would never find out if he sent it from his office in Osaka.

When the fire died down, Hideki stood up, pulled the empty boxes a little farther away, and walked back to the house. He held Shizuko's sketchbook in his hand, keeping it away from his body. Hanae would be in the bedroom getting ready for sleep. Before he went to her, he stopped in his study and deposited the sketchbook in the bottom desk drawer and locked it up. He had no desire to look through it.

In the bedroom, Hanae was sitting in front of her three-way mirror in her short white nightgown and applying cold cream to her face. Her hair·was pulled back and tucked under a white towel. There was another towel draped over her shoulders. With her fingers, she made careful circular movements around her eyes, nose, cheeks. When she took her hand away, her face looked peaceful and blank.

"I left the fire to die down by itself. It should be all right," Hideki said. He sat down on their large, pink-covered futon.

Hanae continued to look into the mirror while she spoke. "It was very good of you. I'm sorry you had to do a chore after your long day at the office. But you know how I don't like to handle fire."

"I left the boxes in the yard," Hideki said. "They wouldn't have burned very well. The ground was damp."

"That's all right. I can use the boxes again. There are plenty of other things I want to throw out."

Hideki stretched out his legs and lay back, facing the ceiling, his arms folded underneath his head.

"I'll be done with this in a minute," Hanae said. "Then I'll bring you some whiskey and give you a massage."

Hideki got up, changed into his pajamas, and lay down again.

He lay flat on his stomach while Hanae straddled his buttocks and her strong, thin hands kneaded his back, over and below his shoulder blades, up and down his sides over his ribs. Her legs braced his waist. With his arms stretched down his sides, his fingertips lightly touched her bare feet. When she was done, he began to drift into sleep. He turned over and felt her lift the covers and crawl in next to him, adjust her head underneath his armpit so her hard little skull was snuggled against the cup of his shoulder.

It must have been two or three in the morning when he woke up staring into the dark closet. Behind him, the white glare of the night lamp flashed on and he heard Hanae's voice.

"What are you doing?" she said.

He let go of the doorknob. "I don't know," he said. "I suppose I wanted to get up and go to the bathroom."

"You've got the wrong door." Hanae waited till he found the door of the bedroom and snapped off the light.

In the hallway, Hideki thought, I must have been too tired to know where I was going. He was sweating profusely. His pajamas felt damp. There was a sour taste in his mouth.

After he washed out his mouth at the sink, he washed his face several times and rubbed it with a towel till his cheeks were red. Now he was too awake to go back to sleep. He turned off the bathroom light and stood in the dark. Something was weighing on his mind, but he couldn't tell what it was. It reminded him vaguely of when he was a young boy, waking up in the middle of the night keenly afraid of having to die someday, wondering what death was like. Surely I cannot be afraid of that now, he told himself. He had gotten over that fear a long time ago, in his twenties, when he became sure that there was nothing beyond this life. The whole time he was in the hospital with tuberculosis, he did not once worry about dying.

His eyes having adjusted to the dark, he walked slowly down the hallway toward his study without turning on the light. He would get some whiskey and read until he was sleepy again. Once in the study, he leaned over his desk to reach out and turn on the desk lamp. The light flashed into his face. He flinched and shut his eyes against its sudden brightness. His vision burned with jagged white lines. He slumped into his chair, breathing hard. His hands shook a little as he took out the desk key, opened the drawer, and pulled out the sketchbook. After a moment's hesitation, he opened it.

The first few pictures were familiar. They were watercolors of the view from the hospital window, of himself lying in bed, of the tulips somebody must have sent him, of a cluttered tray of hospital food that he had refused to eat. A third of the way through the book, watercolors gave way to pencil sketches. They were mostly of Yuki in various stages of her infancy and early childhood—at the harbor, in the park, or at home with her toys on the floor. Hideki tried to imagine the two of them, Yuki absorbed in some toy, Shizuko making a quick sketch of her before she grew restless and began to move again. Day after day, Shizuko had watched her daughter and never tired of sketching her. Hideki quickly glanced through the pages. Toward the end, there was another watercolor. He recognized the small cottage in the mountains where they had spent a few days one summer. That must have been the last vacation he had spent with her. In the sketch, Yuki was standing at the door in a white blouse and pink shorts. She must have been about seven. Hideki tried to remember something about that vacation. There was a small farm nearby where they raised milk cows and sheep, the only farm of that kind in the whole Kobe district. Surely I must have taken them to the farm, he thought. He turned the page and saw a sketch of cows, with Yuki standing gingerly a few yards away from them.

He glanced through the next few watercolors, more cows, sheep, flowers, and came to the second-to-last page. It was a portrait of Yuki, with her long hair in two braids, red ribbons tied around each. She was smiling, holding a bunch of daisies to her face. Hideki didn't know when that was done. During the vacation it must have been. He could not remember when he had last seen Yuki smile.

Hurriedly, he turned to the last page and saw a pencil sketch of himself sleeping in a chair inside the cottage. The chair was a chaise longue made of green canvas. He could almost feel its taut stretch against his back. Leaning over the picture, he found thin petals pressed onto the page. They were the color of ink smudges, four petals connected into one flower. At least ten flowers were scattered over the sketch. Hideki remembered what they were—hydrangea blossoms. These small individual flowers clustered into huge balls that looked like balloons on the foggy mountain paths.

As he looked at the dried petals, he remembered that vacation. On the second day, he and Shizuko had argued about something and he had walked off away from the cottage. In the end, after several hours, he returned with large clusters of hydrangea flowers that he had picked while wandering about the mountain paths all by himself, at first sullen and then sorry, very sorry. He had stuck the flowers almost into Shizuko's face, said something about their being blue rather than pink because it was or wasn't humid, and then sat on the chaise longue hoping that she would now go on as though nothing had happened. And she did. She took the flowers from him, put them in a large pitcher of water, and asked him whether they should go out to supper at a resort hotel nearby. She never referred to their quarrel. Smiling, she turned to Yuki, who looked frightened, and told her to look at the flowers, how the hydrangea changed colors depending on the level of moisture in the soil. That was how she was at her best—gentle, quiet, always considerate about saving his feelings. In all their time together, she had never raised her voice at him or walked away to slam doors and to sulk. When he knew she had forgiven him, he fell asleep in the chair, tired from walking about all day. She must have sketched him then and pressed these flowers into the last page of her sketchbook.

He wanted to remember her as she was that afternoon. He closed and opened his eyes many times, trying. But it was no use. In the harsh light of the desk lamp, he was staring at the brittle flowers, the memory escaping him and leaving him nothing but faded ink smudges. He closed the sketchbook and locked it up again in his desk drawer. Then he remained seated for a long time, his elbows against the edge of the desk, holding his head in his hands like a burden.

14

After the Rain
(August 1975)

The morning after the rainstorm, Masa was out in her garden at five thirty. The two-week drought had gotten her in the habit of rising early to water her plants. Walking through the garden—first the vegetable plots and then the flower beds—she noticed that the wind had knocked down two of her tomato plants. Otherwise, there was little damage.

Masa was in the south corner of the garden, where her white statice and baby's breath had been. Last week, the white flowers had grown into round clusters bigger than her best watermelons. Walking amidst them, she had imagined herself among clouds, the vigorous clouds that towered in the southern sky in mid-summer. But she had harvested the flowers the previous afternoon when the radio warned of the oncoming storm. Now there were only rows and rows of green leaves flat against the muddy ground, looking like wilted lettuce. The flowers were hanging upside down in the shed. In a few weeks, her daughter-in-law, Etsuko, would come from Himeji to pick them up in her car. Etsuko made wreaths and basket decorations out of dried flowers and sold them to a woman who ran a gift shop. Masa grew the flowers for her because Etsuko and Saburo lived on a crowded city street where the eaves of one house practically touched the eaves of the next. Masa had tried to help Etsuko weave the wreaths one year, but her fingers were too stiff for that kind of work now; her eyes, too, even though she saw perfectly well, tired easily from looking at the small, star-shaped flowers of the statice.

It was a wonder that the flowers came back every year. Stuck to the ground, the muddy leaves did not seem to have any life in them. Still, early next spring, every statice and baby's breath would send up long spikes that gradually became thick with blossoms.

Masa remembered a time when she found comfort in the return of various flowers each spring. During the winter months, she used to remind herself of the perennials she had tended over the years, the flowering trees that were older than most of her children. She looked forward eagerly to the first flowers—plums in February, violets in March, cherry blossoms in early April. All that had changed. The spring after Shizuko's death, the lavenders Shizuko had helped her to plant bloomed profusely. The yellow roses Shizuko had built an arch for bloomed for the first time that June. Masa knew then that there was no comfort in the flowers coming back every spring. Until that year, she had planted very few annuals because she hated to see them bloom all summer and die in the fall. The only annuals she and her husband planted every year had been the morning glories that Takeo tended, but every fall, he collected their seeds to plant next spring, so it was more as though the same flowers were coming back after a short rest. Since Shizuko's death, though, Masa planted more annuals—pansies and petunias, sweet peas, impatiens, zinnias.

Some years, the white petunias bloomed into late October, till one morning, the frost snapped them into small, wilted piles.

Masa walked slowly toward the house, stopping now and then to snip off dead leaves or fading flowers, pull out the weeds growing between the plants. There were few weeds. The drought had killed those that had sprung up after Yuki's visit. Yuki had spent hours of her two-week visit weeding the flower beds and vegetable plots. Masa wondered if Yuki had spent so much time outside because she wanted to avoid talking to her.

But Yuki must have been anxious to see us, Masa told herself. She had visited in the last weeks of June, as soon as her college was out for the summer. She said she wanted to stay longer but couldn't because she had to work. Besides, she needed to use the studio at her college for photography and she had to go to the library to read.

"Why do you have to read books or even go to college to study art?" Masa had asked her. "I thought you would be able to learn just from doing it on your own. Isn't that how all the great artists learned? They didn't go to college."

Yuki shook her head. "That was a different time, and a lot of them were apprenticed to other artists even then. They didn't just teach themselves everything. It's hard to explain."

"I was thinking you could live with us here all year round and still be an artist. This is a nice quiet place to live. Why not?"

"I don't know. How would I support myself here?"

"You wouldn't have to worry about that. Grandpa's pension is enough for all three of us if we live modestly. If you want to work, you can always give lessons."

"But I don't want to spend a long time looking at kids' drawings."

"You can coach the track team at the village school. Even people around here read about you in the papers last year when you won those competitions."

"I don't want to coach track teams."

"What will you do after you graduate, anyway? Will you become a teacher somewhere else then?"

"Grandma, I don't know." Yuki sighed. "I just started college. I don't know what I'll do afterward."

"What is the use of going to college if you don't know what you're going there for?"

"Maybe I'm going *because* I don't know. I just want to study art now. I have no idea about four years from now or even next year. I don't want to think that far ahead."

Masa was going to point out that this was too haphazard a way to live when Yuki abruptly stood up and put on her straw hat.

"I'm going to the garden. I didn't weed your petunia patch yet," she said. "Let me know if there's something else I can do."

Yuki was never rude or irritable on this visit. Even when they disagreed, her face was always full of patience. But something was wrong. Masa felt a strain when they talked, and she was sure that Yuki felt it also. So much of it, she thought, was Yuki's father's fault. If he had allowed Yuki to visit regularly, things would have been different. As it was, Masa felt that Yuki had suddenly become somebody else—a tall and thin girl, a young woman almost, whose face was full of patience.

168

When Yuki was a child, it was Masa herself whose face had had that look. Now, it had somehow become the other way around, with no gradual change to explain it, nothing in between.

Masa crouched down to examine the three-colored violas planted by the side of the house. The rain did not seem to have helped them much. Their leaves were still turning brown, most of their buds drying out rather than blossoming. The few flowers that had opened were stunted looking. Gently lifting the thick foliage, Masa found a fine web among the lower stems and knew what was causing the violas to wither. The web, fine as dust, was a sign of spider mites that had infested her other plants in previous years. The mites lived on the juices they sucked from stems and buds. Smaller than flecks of dust, their bodies were reddish orange, almost ruby, almost beautiful.

Masa looked up from the violas and saw Takeo walking out of the front door, on his way to the hen coop to collect the eggs. As he waved at her, she got up and continued to examine the flowers. When the ground dried a little, she would dust the violas. Perhaps she would be able to catch them in time.

When Takeo woke up a few minutes before six that same morning, Masa had already risen. Her thin body seemed to leave no warmth or wrinkles on the futon bedding. Takeo lay on his back and stared at the ceiling.

He could still hear children's voices from his dreams. He had dreamed of hundreds of schoolchildren running in a field of pampas grass. Some of them, he knew, were children he had never seen. Others had been his students during his forty years as a schoolteacher. Then scattered among them were his children and grandchildren. How can I pick out my own children among all these? he had wondered helplessly in the dream. That was just before he woke up. His ear still echoed with their voices—hundreds of children all speaking in twos and threes, their voices making noises like the wind in the long grass.

Lately, waking or sleeping, Takeo heard distant noises that sometimes sounded like the wind, other times like children's voices. The noises were never loud. They didn't prevent him from hearing other things. But several times during the day he noticed the constant echo.

He wondered if this was an indication that he was losing his hearing. Even though the echo in his ear was not a serious problem now, it might come to interfere with his hearing later on. He thought of the old man and the old woman across the road, only ten or twelve years older than himself. They had been deaf for seven or eight years now. He saw them sometimes on his walks, their hands fluttering like excited birds. Once, about two years ago, he was planting his only rice paddy, which lay across the road next to the couple's house. The old man and the old woman were in their yard, arguing, it seemed, about how to stake out their plots. Takeo was startled by their voices. Low, blunted moans spilled from their mouths while their hands did the real talking. He realized for the first time that both of them being deaf, the man and the woman no longer used their spoken words. The sounds that came out of their mouths now had no shape or meaning. They had forgotten how to speak.

It seemed especially horrible that the woman across

170

the road, who had been so talkative, had become deaf and mute. Both the man and the woman had grown up in the village in the days before the land reform, when Takeo's family owned all the land east of the river. Even now, when Takeo met them in the street, the man and the woman bowed deeply to him as though he were their landlord. If he bowed back, they bowed even deeper. Until the year she became deaf, the woman had brought over to Takeo and Masa the best of her crops— the largest, ripest watermelon, beautiful tomatoes, cucumbers, eggplant, bunch after bunch of flowers. She would stay and talk with Masa, telling her the problems of her family, asking for advice, as though Masa were still the landowner's wife, the most influential woman in the village. Takeo had tried to discourage the woman from bringing the gifts. But she only said, "Our family always brought the best to yours. Your mother gave my mother such helpful advice." When Takeo was troubled by her gifts, Masa only smiled. "But everybody in the village feels the injustice even though they benefited from it," she said. "They think that the land shouldn't have been taken away from us quite so abruptly. They felt bad when they saw you working at the school all day and farming in the evenings to make ends meet. It makes them feel better to show you the same respect as before." "But you know the land reform had to happen," he said to Masa—just as he had taught his students. "Our country couldn't have gone on after the War with only a few people owning the land. It wasn't a very productive system. People are more motivated when the land they work belongs to them. Besides, I enjoyed being a schoolteacher. I wouldn't have liked sitting in my big house and nodding to my tenant farmers

171

as they brought in their rent. I wouldn't have wanted to see them live on millet or oats while I ate white rice every day."

Takeo rose and put on his brown haori jacket over the long shirt and underwear he had slept in. Then he went to the Buddhist altar in the family room. Masa had already brought the daily offering of rice and tea in the small white cups she used for the altar. After her work in the garden, she would come in with a fresh bunch of zinnias or chrysanthemums for the altar.

He lit an incense stick and closed his eyes. His head bowed, he tried to forget the constant chatter of his mind and be at peace as he faced the altar. The distant echo of children's voices faded gradually. For a brief moment, his mind was almost blank, peaceful. Then he was thinking again of his children and grandchildren, the woman across the road, his family losing the land, the rainstorm during the night, Shizuko, Yuki, Masa . . . It was impossible to concentrate on being at peace. He had thought once that it would be easier as he grew older.

How wrong I was, he thought as he opened his eyes.

The bright blues, purples and green of the fabric on the altar flooded his thoughts. Yuki had dyed the cloth during her visit and left it on the altar as an offering to the spirits. Its design, showing a cluster of irises, was made up of various shades of blue—some of them closer to green, others closer to purple.

Shizuko's colors, Takeo had thought as soon as Yuki had finished the cloth.

When he looked at the irises now, he knew again that Yuki was going to be all right. It was something he could not quite explain, even to Masa, who worried so much. As soon as Yuki showed him the cloth dyed in the colors her mother had loved, Takeo knew that Yuki would find her way. She was beginning to look beyond the sadness and pain her mother's memory must still bring her.

Takeo stood up slowly, leaving the incense to burn down by itself. He went through the house toward the front door. His legs had been better since the warm weather. He was practicing walking without his cane again, though he could not walk fast. Exercise was good. He would go and collect the eggs from the hen coop. The woven basket for the eggs hung on the nail near the door. The sun shone through it and cast a latticework shadow on the wall.

Outside, Masa was among the violas planted against the house. He waved to her and walked toward the hen coop. The ground smelled of rain. He could see already that it would be a hot day. By noon, the rain of the night before would be rising in vapors from the hot ground and the cicadas would be droning in the trees, their voices like currents of heat.

The hens were quiet this morning. None tried to escape or peck at his fingers while he gathered the eggs, still warm, out of the straw. His son, Saburo, had come to butcher the rooster one afternoon during Yuki's visit. The rooster had been getting too mean. Yuki asked her uncle, dead serious, if he couldn't just let the rooster wander off. No, Masa had to explain. It would only stay in the garden pecking at all her flowers. Yuki stayed in the house while her uncle butchered the rooster in the yard. She didn't come out for a long time. Somehow, it made Takeo smile to think about it.

For all Masa's worries, Yuki had not changed all that much. When she was about eight years old and she and her mother were visiting for the summer, Saburo went fishing one afternoon and returned with two buckets full of bass. Masa cooked the fish for supper. Yuki, having seen her uncle scale the fish, would not eat them. She made herself a lettuce sandwich instead—lettuce and peanut butter together on toasted bread, which Saburo said was more disgusting than any kind of dead fish. "At least the lettuce wasn't scaled while it was jumping around," Yuki retorted. During her recent visit, she said that she had become a vegetarian. "A friend of mine went to help some farmers butcher pigs because he thought that since he ate pork, he ought to be able to kill the pigs himself," she said. "That made a lot of sense. I stopped eating any kind of meat or fish because I could never kill anything." That was just like Yuki, to think like that. She still ate lettuce and peanut butter sandwiches. One night, Takeo saw her making them as a late-night snack. She even offered to make one for him. When he declined, saying that he still didn't feel up to such a strange combination of food, she replied, "Grandpa, it's good for you," as though he were a child now and she a mother. It had made him laugh.

Takeo collected the last egg and went out of the hen coop. Since the rooster had been gone, Masa said that she heard one of the hens crowing almost like a rooster. She must be mistaken, Takeo decided. He had heard nothing of the kind.

As he walked toward the house, he could see his wife cutting some zinnias from the patch closer to the road. The zinnias had done well this year. Some of them were unusual colors—salmon, lavender, peach.

He stepped inside the house and waited a few seconds for his eyes to adjust. The echo of the children's voices returned, a little louder than when he had gotten up. From the hallway, he could see the wooden slide in the sun porch. He had built it when Shizuko was born.

That was forty-six years ago, he thought. Shizuko would have been forty-six years old if she had lived. He felt a sudden sadness. There was nothing he would have liked more, he thought, than to hear Shizuko complain about white strands in her hair, about her laugh lines deepening. But she had not lived long enough to be concerned about such things. They would never be laughing together about getting old.

He walked to the kitchen and was about to put down the basket of eggs on the table when the pain came. It was almost as though something, a small hand, was scratching the walls of his chest. He stood motionless, looking at the basket of eggs in his hand. Then the pain became sharper. It started somewhere between his chest and stomach and spread both upward and downward.

Behind him, the door opened. Masa was coming into the house. He wanted to turn around and look at her coming down the hallway, pink and purple zinnias in her hand. But his chest hurt too much. He had to stand still and concentrate on the pain. Masa, he wanted to say, don't worry. Don't grieve. But he could not utter a sound.

Slowly, he leaned forward and managed to put down the basket of eggs on the table. Then he stood looking at them, eight eggs nestled in the woven basket. When the rooster had been there, Takeo had candled the eggs. Most of them had lit up completely in front of the flame, light flooding out the thin shell. Each egg was a perfect sphere of light in the arc of his hand.

Masa was saying something behind him. He could

not hear clearly. The echo in his ears became louder. For the first time, it seemed to block out his hearing.

Masa tossed the bunch of zinnias on the table. The flowers scattered over the basket of eggs.

Zinnias for the altar, Takeo thought. Thank you, Masa. He tried to smile. The flowers are for me. They are beautiful.

Yuki was about to leave for work when the telephone rang. She had already put on her waitress uniform. Her friend Isamu was going to give her a ride on his motorcycle to the restaurant where she worked. She asked him to wait in her room while she answered the phone in the hallway. None of the other boarders were home.

The first thing she heard when she picked up the phone was her grandmother's voice saying, "Your grandfather's had a heart attack."

Yuki was speechless. Her grandmother hadn't waited for Yuki to identify herself or even to say "Hello." She wondered, for a moment, what she might have done if any of the other boarders had picked up the phone. Then she realized the full meaning of what her grandmother was saying.

"Is he all right?" Yuki asked.

"No." Her grandmother said nothing more.

"What do you mean, no?" Yuki shouted. She was stunned by the loudness of her own voice.

"How soon can you come for the funeral?"

Yuki heard the scratchy sound of the static and realized that she was gripping the telephone cord, twisting it hard.

"You can come, can't you?"

"I'll be there on the first train tomorrow morning."

Yuki had a feeling of listening to someone else's voice. "I have to go to work right now. Then I don't have to work till the day after tomorrow—maybe not then, either. I'll try to switch off with one of the other girls."

"Why can't you come tonight?"

"I was on my way to work. It's too late to call in."

"Is that so important at a time like this?"

Yuki stopped for a moment. What's the hurry now? a voice said inside her. What good would anything do? "I'll come the first thing in the morning. I'm sorry, Grandma. I can't afford to call in at the last minute and get fired. But I'll be there soon. Wait for me, okay?"

As she hung up, she thought of the telephone call six years ago, when she called her grandmother after her mother's death. She had to repeat herself because her grandmother wouldn't hear it. Finally, her grandmother said, "Is this one of your tricks?" so that Yuki had to repeat, "No. I'm telling the truth. Mama's dead." She hung up. Her grandmother called back and said, "Your grandfather and I are leaving right away. We'll be there before midnight. I'll call your aunt Aya and make sure she gets there soon too. Just wait for us." Her grandparents' train was delayed. Yuki fell asleep before they arrived. She woke up the next morning and found her grandmother in the kitchen waiting to make her breakfast.

Isamu was standing in the hallway, looking at her.

"Are you all right?" he asked. "What was that all about?"

"My grandfather just died," Yuki said. "I have to leave in the morning."

"Your grandfather?"

"My grandfather I went to see in June."

"I'm sorry. Are you all right?"

"I don't know." Yuki walked toward her room, where she had left her purse and her waitress shoes. "I just can't believe it," she said. "I should have seen him more often."

Isamu put his hand on her shoulder as if to stop her. "Maybe you shouldn't go to work."

Yuki continued to walk, so he had to let go. "I can't skip work on short notice," she said. She went into her room, picked up her purse and shoes, and turned to Isamu. "We should go."

His motorcycle was parked in front of the boarding-house. She sat behind him and put her arms lightly around his waist.

"You have to really hold on, remember?" he said. "Last time, you were so busy looking around, you almost let go."

"Okay."

When the motorcycle started, the wind whistled in her ears. Isamu sped up, and the whistle turned into a louder noise, like the noise of a waterfall.

I should have seen him more often, she kept repeating to herself. She remembered her recent visit, how she had argued with her grandmother and gone to the garden, pretending to be so interested in weeding the flower patches. Why didn't I spend more time with him then and before? she thought; I should have visited him no matter what my father said. Her mind was stuck on that regret. She couldn't think of anything else. She couldn't even cry.

"Yuki!" Isamu was shouting above the noise of the wind. "I told you to hold on! You're about to let go and fall off."

"I'm sorry." She leaned forward and tightened her arms around him. "I know I shouldn't let go."

Isamu pulled his motorcycle to the curb in front of the restaurant and turned off the engine. Yuki got off.

"Can I pick you up after work?" he asked.

"You don't have to do that. I can get a ride from someone here."

"Let me take you to the station tomorrow morning, then."

"All right. Thanks." She turned to go.

"Wait," he said. He got off the motorcycle and stood in front of her. "Call me after work," he said. "You know you can call me anytime if you want to talk."

"I know," she said. "Thank you."

He reached over and squeezed her shoulder. "I'll be thinking of you," he said. "Hang in there."

She smiled at him and went into the dark foyer of the restaurant.

At seven o'clock, the restaurant was at its busiest. Yuki had several tables of couples and families, and a large group of businessmen who all wanted mixed drinks and separate checks. She was going to get the third round of drinks for the businessmen when the busboy tapped her arm. "Those people over there," he said, pointing to one of the families. "They want their check."

"Well, they'll have to wait," she said, and continued toward the bar. She didn't have the checks figured out. She would have to do it leaning on the bar while the bartender mixed the drinks.

At the bar, she ordered the drinks and then pulled the bunch of checks out of her apron pocket. She began to leaf through them for the family's check. It was hard to read her own handwriting in the dim light from the bar. She always wrote too small, the lines bunched together too tight. Her grandfather had tried to teach her to write more neatly when she was a child. He would write down some numbers and letters on the dotted lines of her notebook and she would try to make her own as much like his as possible. As she looked at her cramped-up handwriting, she thought again, Why didn't I go on seeing him after Mama's death, when he would have wanted to see me all the more?

"Hey." The busboy was behind her again. "Those people. They're really anxious for their check. They asked me to get it for them."

At the same time, the bartender, in the middle of mixing one of the drinks, said, "Two martinis, two gin and tonics, a Manhattan, two tequila sunrises, what else? Did you say whiskey sour cocktail or whiskey and sour?"

"I can't remember," Yuki said.

"What do you mean, you can't remember? That's your job."

The busboy repeated, "Did you hear me? The check."

"Leave me alone," Yuki said. Everyone at the bar turned around. "Both of you. Leave me alone."

The bartender stopped in the midst of making the second tequila sunrise. The grenadine continued to drip into the glass, each drop of red blooming toward the bottom.

Flowers floated into Yuki's memory. Large flowers like watercolor splashes. Her grandfather's morning glories had come in more colors than anybody else's. Every fall, he saved the seeds, labeling each package in his beautiful handwriting about the color and the year

180

and the size of the flowers so that the morning glories would continue, huge splashes of color climbing over the fence.

The bartender was staring at her.

"My grandfather died this afternoon," she said. Her voice was thick and her throat hurt.

"Take a break, Yuki; it's all right," she heard the bartender saying. "Those people can wait. Go onto the balcony. There's no one out there."

She turned away from the bar and hurried onto the balcony. She walked to the far end and stood watching the white and yellow lights of downtown, a few miles away. The low sky above them was streaked with their reflections. Her grandparents' house seemed so far away. There, the countryside would be completely dark now, the miles of flooded rice paddies like a calm sea. During her visit, she had sat in that darkness with her grandfather, listening to the early crickets. She had imagined the stars above them making the same sounds, light-years away. Her grandfather had said that watching the stars with her, when she was a little girl, was one of his best memories. Yuki looked up from the glimmer of city lights to the dark sky, which was too hazy for stars. On the road below the balcony, cars were driving by, their wheels making a swishing sound like water flowing down a long river. Yuki stayed alone on the balcony for a long time listening to the sounds.

15
The Effects of Light
(August 1975)

The chives planted outside the window at Isamu's boardinghouse had flowered in the four days Yuki was with her grandmother. Their purple heads stuck out above the narrow green leaves. Isamu was making some coffee. Yuki sat at the table to examine the three black-and-white photographs he had taken of her the day before she left. In the background, she could see the field outside Nagasaki where they had had a picnic lunch. All three photographs showed her standing in that field and laughing. Anybody who saw them would think she looked happy. At the time, she had had no idea that her grandfather was dying.

Yuki put away the photographs and watched as Isamu poured the boiling water over the coffee grounds. In his blue T-shirt and jeans, he looked tall and thin, reminding her of the shadows the moonlight made from poplars and cedars. The first time they met, on the first day of school at the college library, he was standing by the window with a large photography book in his hands. He looked serious, almost sad. But then he closed the book, smiled at Yuki, and said, "Hi. I'm Isamu Nagano. Who are you? You must be a new student." A year ahead of her in school, Isamu had grown up in Nagasaki, though his parents now lived on the main island. In April and May, he showed her the city and the countryside around it. Since school got out in June, he had been teaching her how to use his camera and develop her own film. They went to parks, beaches, the mountainside to shoot pictures. They could go almost anywhere on his motorcycle.

When the coffee was ready, Isamu handed her one of the cups and asked, "Do you want to sit in the garden?"

"Yes, that sounds nice." Yuki stood up. She was tired after her all-night train ride. When she called Isamu from the station at six, the sun had just come up. Now, it was past nine and the garden looked sunny and warm.

Yuki left her travel bag in the kitchen and went out the back door to the stone bench in the back of the garden. Isamu had brought his camera. He aimed it at his landlady's dahlias, but put it away without shooting. The dahlias were bright pink. Blue and yellow delphiniums towered behind them.

"The garden's at its best, isn't it?" Yuki said as they sat side by side drinking coffee. "This is such a nice place to sit and see the flowers." Because his landlady was an old friend of his mother's, Isamu was free to use the kitchen and sit in the garden, privileges most boarders didn't have.

"You can come here anytime," he said, "even if I'm not home. I'll tell my landlady." He poured her more coffee from the thermos. "So are you all right?" he asked.

She nodded. "But I'm worried about my grandmother. She's never been alone in her life. My uncle Saburo lives close enough to help, but I'm worried she'll be lonely."

Isamu put his hand on her back. "Things will work out."

His hand was warm. He patted her shoulder and then rested his palm against the nape of her neck. She stood up abruptly and walked back and forth in front of the dahlias. Her steps stirred up some brownish grasshoppers. They flew low to the ground, their wings vibrating. She stopped in front of the bench and sat down on the grass.

"So tell me what you've been doing," she said, trying to sound cheerful.

"Let's see," he said, smiling—still, in the way his eyes narrowed, she knew he was hurt by her abruptness. While he talked, she picked at the grass and the fallen twigs around her until she realized she was making a small pile of broken stems and leaves. She scattered them again. She couldn't help thinking of the way people at work teased her about him. "No, he's not my boyfriend," she would insist, her face feeling hot. "He's my best friend. That's better. I don't want him to be a boyfriend."

At ten, she got up to leave. "I have to go to work. I should drop off my bag and get my uniform."

"I'll give you a ride," he said.

"No, it's only a few blocks."

"How about getting to the restaurant?"

"One of the other waitresses picks me up when I work during lunch. She'll be there."

"I'll walk with you to your place, then." When Isamu stood up, his camera fell on the ground. He sat back down and picked it up. "The shoulder strap's broken."

"Let's see." Yuki sat down next to him. She took the

camera and put it on her lap. She could see where the black leather strap had slipped free.

"There should be a buckle that holds this together. It must have just come off."

He leaned forward over the ground, looked, and then found the small metal clasp. She put the camera back on his lap.

"Here, you do it," she said. "It's your camera. You want to know how to fix it in case this happens again."

"Do I?"

"Watch." She picked up one end of the strap and put it into his right hand. Next, she hooked the buckle onto the other end and placed it in his left hand. "Look, the strap goes under and over the buckle and hooks on the other end. Just like a belt. See that?" Yuki put her right hand over his, trying to guide him. "No." She drew back her hand. "Hold that buckle steady. Don't move it around like that."

"To tell you the truth," he said, turning sideways to look into her face, "this is kind of distracting. I'm not exactly thinking about the camera." He put his arm around her shoulders and drew her closer. "I thought about you a lot," he said, "while you were gone."

She stood up, her heart beating fast. But when he reached up and took her hand, she didn't pull back. He turned her palm toward him and put his lips lightly to her wrist. She hesitated, half wanting to sit down. He looked so serious, a little sad even. Neither of them spoke. Finally, she drew back her hand very gently so he had to let go. The next moment, she was walking away. She didn't turn around until she was in the neighbor's yard, too far to see his face clearly. He was still sitting on the bench. The camera had fallen on the ground again.

"I'll call you after work!" she shouted. "I'll see you later."

She cut across the yard to the street and ran back to her boardinghouse. Standing in front of her door with the keys in hand, she realized she had left her bag in his landlady's kitchen.

At twelve thirty, when every table but one was occupied, a regular customer, Mr. Sato, came in and stood at the door. The hostess went to seat him. The two of them took a few steps away from the door and then stopped. They talked for a long time. Yuki could see them looking in her direction now and then as she waited on her tables. In the end, Mr. Sato went back to stand at the door, to wait for a different table, Yuki guessed. The only unoccupied table was in her section. As she walked back to the kitchen to pick up her order, she felt satisfied, almost proud, that Mr. Sato would not sit in her section. She didn't care what he said to the hostess to avoid taking that table. She wouldn't have waited on him even if he had sat there.

About a month ago, Mr. Sato came in for lunch at two thirty, almost stumbling from being drunk. Because he was a regular customer, the hostess seated him though it was near the end of lunchtime and the few customers still at the tables were getting ready to leave. After Yuki took his order, Mr. Sato dropped his fork and signaled to her. She brought him a clean fork and was about to put it down in front of him when he reached and grabbed her other hand. He squeezed her fingers. Yuki brought the fork back up, held it next to his nose, and said, "Let go right now. This should be sharp enough to break your skin." She didn't raise her voice because she felt perfectly calm, though very angry. Mr. Sato let go immediately. Nobody saw or heard the exchange except Kazuko, one of the other waitresses, who happened to be nearby, cleaning up her tables.

"You've got nerve," Kazuko said. "I'd have gotten all flustered and nervous if he had done that to me."

Yuki had shrugged. "It didn't bother me that much," she said. She didn't feel nervous when she was angry but in the right. When his order came up, she brought it to his table and said, "This is absolutely the last time I will wait on you." Mr. Sato still came back to the restaurant for lunch occasionally, but he never sat in her section.

As Yuki stepped out of the kitchen with a tray full of plates, Mr. Sato turned to stare at her from the doorway. She stared back until he looked away, and wished there was an adult version of sticking out your tongue at people so she could show him her contempt.

Putting two cups of coffee on the tray along with the dishes, Yuki thought again about what had happened this morning. It was completely different from her run-in with Mr. Sato. She could still hear Isamu's voice saying, "I'm not exactly thinking about the camera." His eyes were saying, I'm thinking of you, isn't it obvious? He had looked at her that way several times before, but not as clearly as this morning. Her heart beat faster when she remembered how he put his arm around her shoulders. They were so close she could feel the words starting up in his throat before he said them. "I thought a lot about you," he had said. His words had upset her because she, too, had thought a lot about him while she was gone. Between the times when she was sad about her grandfather or worried about her grandmother, Yuki had wondered what Isamu would think of the green paddies outside, her grandmother's purple lantern flowers and the wooden slide her grandfather had built, the finches their neighbor kept in bamboo cages. When she talked to Mr. Kimura, she wished Isamu was there to meet him. They would have liked each other, she was sure. She thought of the way Isamu held her hand and kissed her wrist this morning. She had wanted to sit down next to him and say, "I thought a lot about you, too."

But I don't want to fall in love, she reminded herself. She put the tray down on the table and placed the food in front of two women—a mother and a daughter, no doubt. They both had big paper bags as if they had been shopping all morning. Yuki asked them if they needed anything. No, they shook their heads, nothing. They looked a lot alike when they smiled. Yuki turned to go. What I need, she told herself, is friendship, not love. Isamu is my best friend. I should be satisfied with that. Besides, she thought, love ends in sadness one way or another—I don't want any more sadness.

When she got home from work, she found a note on the door from one of the other boarders: *Isamu called,* it said. *call him back.* She took down the note and put it in her pocket. A flat, square package had been left by the door where the landlady put Yuki's mail. Yuki went into her room and sat on the bed with the package. There were stamps on it, but no return address. She tore the brown wrapping and threw it on the floor.

188

Inside, she found a large notebook with a bright sky-blue cover. Immediately, she thought of her mother. It was one of the colors her mother had loved. She had a notebook like this for her pencil sketches and watercolors.

Yuki opened the notebook in the middle and found a sketch of a park. A little girl in a straw hat was feeding some pigeons by a water fountain. Yuki could almost feel the tight weave of that straw hat; it had a long pink ribbon that fluttered in the wind when she and her mother walked in the park and sat by the fountain. She picked up the torn paper from the floor. The stamps had been canceled two days ago at a post office in western Osaka; that would be the post office closest to her father's office.

Her father had been notified of her grandfather's death. Her uncle Saburo had sent him a telegram even before Yuki's arrival. "He was our son-in-law," her grandmother said. "He shouldn't have to find out from someone else. That would be an embarrassment to him. People would say he had given us cause for resentment and that's why he wasn't notified. I don't want to embarrass him that way." On the day of the funeral, her father didn't call or send a telegram. Even in the next three days, no flowers or note of condolence came from him.

"I'm ashamed to be his daughter," Yuki had said.

"It's not your fault," her grandmother said. She didn't say, "Don't say things like that about your own father," or "Maybe he has some good reason."

If her father had a good reason, it would be that he never got the telegram. But Yuki was sure now that he had gotten the telegram and found out about her grandfather's death. He had sent the sketchbook to her two days after. He must have thought it would somehow make up for not sending his condolences to her grandmother. But he didn't write her a note or even put his name on the package. It was almost as though the sketchbook had come back to her on its own and he had nothing to do with it. He's wrong to think this makes up for anything, Yuki thought as she opened the first page.

The first set of pictures were watercolors. The dates penciled in the corners were from before her birth or even her parents' marriage. Still, she remembered looking through them a long time ago with her mother, who stopped after each page to tell the stories of her father's illness. Yuki tried to remember. Here, she thought, was the view from the hospital where her father had spent a year with his tuberculosis. Then there was the tray of lunch he refused to eat because, her mother said, he thought everything at the hospital tasted like throat lozenges. Then the tulips his mother had brought one day, which he didn't like because their bright colors gave him a headache. Yuki's mother had laughed as she told these stories. She was amused by what a terrible, spoiled patient her husband had been.

Yuki peered at the picture of him sleeping on the hospital bed. Her mother had loved him and found his faults amusing. Maybe he was different back then, she thought. Otherwise her mother wouldn't have been at his bedside every day against everyone's advice. Forget him, they told her; he's going to die. She should have forgotten him, Yuki thought now. She should have walked out of the room while he was sleeping and never gone back.

In the middle part of the sketchbook, Yuki saw sketch

after sketch of herself done in pencil. The strokes were swift but careful. In the later pictures, she recognized some of the clothes, toys, places. She remembered the grainy taste of the wooden building blocks, the pink wool cap she had wanted to wear even in the summer, the pier where she had seen ships for the first time. Then she came to a group of watercolors from a vacation she could remember well, when they spent a weekend at a friend's cottage in the mountains near Kobe. She looked through the pictures of the cottage, the flowers outside, the dairy farm her father had taken them to. That was the last weekend her father had spent with them. Yuki was seven, in second grade. She had collected mountain flowers and leaves and pressed them between her mother's books to bring to school in the fall.

On the second-to-last page, Yuki found a detailed watercolor portrait of herself holding some daisies to her nose and smiling a big, frank smile. Her hair was braided and tied with red ribbons. This is how my mother saw me, she thought, such a happy child. Back then, strangers used to smile at her on the bus or in the store when she was with her mother. "You're mama's girl, aren't you?" they would say as she and her mother stood or walked hand in hand. "You're lucky to take after her so." We were happy, Yuki thought; anybody could tell.

She turned to the last page. It was a pencil sketch of her father sleeping on the chaise longue in the cottage. Her mother's pencil strokes were at once bold and careful. She must have been eager to sketch him before he woke up. Several hydrangea blossoms had been pressed right onto the page. The petals were intact, though the color had faded from bright purple to blue.

Yuki went back to the first sketch of her father sleeping in the hospital bed. In both pictures, he looked slightly sullen but almost comical, endearing even—the spoiled patient whose complaints had made her mother laugh. This is how she wanted to see him, Yuki thought as she turned back to the last page, even when I was seven.

The hydrangea blossoms were shaped like round-edged crosses. These, Yuki remembered, were the flowers her father had brought. Her parents had argued for a long time that morning. As usual, her father had shouted, slammed the door, and gone away. But this one time, he came back in the late afternoon and handed the flowers to her mother. He sat down on the chair, looking sheepish and sorry. Then he fell asleep. He must have been relieved. Rather than complaining to him about the way he had walked off, her mother had let him sleep. She even pressed these flowers to the last page of her sketchbook. She must have wanted to remember his gesture of apology, his coming back to her. She must have loved him still.

Yuki closed the sketchbook and put it on the bed. She wondered when her mother had stopped loving her father, what she would say if Yuki could ask her now, "Did you regret loving him?" Mr. Kimura had said in February that he wanted to love someone even if it might end in sadness. At the funeral, he was solicitous toward her aunt Aya; he clearly loved her. But love brings sadness, Yuki thought, even when the other person doesn't hurt you on purpose.

When all the funeral guests had gone home, her

grandmother had sat alone at the Buddhist altar for two hours. Yuki went to join her because she was worried. Her grandmother said, "I'm trying to get used to talking to him this way." She wouldn't go to sleep, though Yuki asked her to. Her grandmother would suffer for months, for years: even the simplest things, like planting petunias in the garden or cooking rice, would remind her of her husband, what he would say or do if he had been with her. Everything and anything could bring on the sadness. Maybe she would have been better off, Yuki thought, if she hadn't loved him in the first place, if she had been alone all along. Still, even while she was witnessing her grandmother's grief, Yuki had kept thinking of Isamu. She had imagined the photographs he would take of the bamboo thickets behind the house, the swift current of the river, the stretches of rice paddies. She had wanted to show him her childhood places: the chestnut tree she had climbed and couldn't come down from, the small stream behind the house where she had watched catfish swimming, the paths between the paddies that were covered with clover. She regretted how he would never be able to meet her grandfather or her mother. They would have liked him, she kept thinking. She couldn't stop.

Yuki picked up the sketchbook again and looked at the various sketches of her childhood. There she was, page after page, stacking up the wooden blocks into a tower so she could smash them down and hear the crash, trying to feed her peaches to her pink teddy bear, sticking her nose against the curved glass of the fishbowl, standing a safe distance away from the cows at the dairy farm because their large white faces frightened her. She could hear the way her mother used to laugh at her. Yuki, you are simply too much, she would say between gasps of laughter; you take everything so to heart.

Soon, Yuki came to the last portrait of herself. It was such a cheerful picture. The white daisies in her hands were painted with bright yellow centers. Her mother had used the same yellow, diluted a little more, to paint the background. It looked like a wash of bright light surrounding the scene. Yuki thought of Isamu again.

On the first day they had gone together to use his camera, he showed her how to focus and center her pictures, how to adjust for light. While he was looking away, she took a picture of a heron wading across a river. "Oh, you need a different lens for that," he said. "That was the next thing I was going to tell you about." When they developed the film, the one of the heron turned out to be her favorite shot anyway. The picture looked almost blank at first glance but was actually filled with gray ripples of shiny water like faint pencil scratches; the heron showed up as a blurred white line at the center. "It's not sour grapes; I really like this," Yuki told Isamu. "It's a good picture," he agreed. "It looks like you were taking a picture of light." That was what she liked about black-and-white photographs: the way they captured the effects of light.

Yuki closed the sketchbook and held it on her lap. My mother, she thought, wanted to be that blurred heron at the center of my mind, almost swallowed up by the light around it but always there. She would want me to look beyond her unhappiness.

She went into the hallway and dialed Isamu's number. He answered right away.

"Hi," she said. "I got off work a while ago." She stopped, feeling almost shy.

"You left your bag," he said. "I didn't mean to upset you and make you forget it. Are you feeling okay?" His voice was warm and kind. "I'm sorry if I did anything to hurt or offend you."

"I'm all right," she said. She thought of him developing her portraits in the lab while she was gone, the gray lines gradually darkening into images, into her laughter.

"You're not offended?" he asked. "I was afraid you'd never call back."

"No," she said. "I wasn't offended at all"—she paused—"or hurt."

They were silent for a while. Finally, she said, "Are you busy right now?"

"No, not at all."

She took a deep breath so her voice would come out steady. "Could you meet me in the park?" she asked. "I want to talk to you."

"Are you sure? I keep thinking you're mad at me."

"Believe me," she said. "I'm not mad." She waited a while and added, "I missed you too, when I was gone."

"I'll meet you in the park in a few minutes," he said. "I'm leaving right now."

Yuki went back to her room and picked up the sketchbook, looked briefly at the last picture of her father, closed the book, and put it in her desk drawer. She wasn't going to write to thank him. She couldn't. It was better to be silent than to lie or be insincere. She couldn't thank him unless she felt real gratitude toward him. Until then, she would say nothing. Maybe I'll show the sketchbook to Isamu, she thought, next time.

I'll remember her with him, and that would be the closest they could come to meeting each other.

She ran out of the room, down the stairs. The park was a block away, between their two boardinghouses. Running down the street, she kept thinking of the various sketches of herself. My mother wanted me to be happy, she repeated to herself. She didn't leave me to hurt me or to make me sad all my life. At the entrance of the park, Yuki slowed down. Isamu was already waiting by the swings. She waved at him and stopped. Seeing her, he picked up her bag and started walking toward her, flicking his feet outward just a little with each step. She had noticed this habit of his when they ran together for the first time in May. "Slow down," he had kept asking her then. "I'm not up to your speed, Yuki. If I had known I was going to meet you, I would have been training all last year to keep up with you." When they were done, he had flopped down on the grass and stretched his arms to the side. "I think I'm going to die," he said. It made her smile to remember that. She stood on the edge of the grass and waited.

"Hey," she called to him. "Hurry up."

He waved to her and smiled. Next time he turned to her with his serious look, she would take his hand and draw closer, then hold still while her heart beat faster. She looked around at the swing set and the slide, the flower beds clustered around walkways. Isamu was still smiling. He was getting ready to say something. As Yuki stepped out onto the grass to meet him, her mind kept taking pictures of the surrounding light.

Epilogue
(May 1976)

On the morning of her seventy-fifth birthday, Masa woke up to the music from the schoolyard, where the neighborhood children were performing eight o'clock calisthenics. Sunlight streaked yellow on the side of the family altar. Masa lay gazing at the painted images of Buddha in his various manifestations. They were in the back of the altar, almost hidden behind the incense burners and unlit candles, spring chrysanthemums in a brass vase, and the small cups in which she offered food and tea to the spirits of her ancestors.

Since her husband Takeo's death, nine months ago, Masa had taken to sleeping in the family room. As soon as she woke up there, no longer in her old bedroom, she remembered that Takeo was gone—she didn't have to forget momentarily and then remind herself as though she had to hear the same sad news over and over. The first thing she saw when she opened her eyes every morning was the Buddhist altar, where she honored the spirits of the ancestors Takeo had joined.

Masa lay thinking about the spirits. Fifty-five years ago, when she was newly married and she began her morning ritual at her husband's family altar, the spirits of the ancestors had seemed like a large white cloud—a nameless benevolent force floating over her. Since then, the spirits had taken more familiar forms: her first-born, who had died of measles before the others were born, another son killed in the War, her parents and parents-in-law. But these days, when she placed food and flowers on the altar, she thought of her husband, Takeo, and her daughter Shizuko. She prayed or talked to these two when she bowed at the altar, where she came to spend more than a minute in silence. The others had joined the general dead, whom she spoke and thought of as "the spirits of my ancestors," but Takeo and Shizuko remained separate, individual in her grief. They were waiting for her, she thought, before the three of them could join the ancestors and merge into the white cloud of peace. She wanted that day to come soon.

When the music from the schoolyard had stopped, Masa rose, wrapped a gray kimono around herself, and began to fold her futon. On the quilted cover of the futon, she could always recognize some of the kimonos that had gone into its making. There was the red silk, the color of ripe strawberries, that her daughters had worn when they were children. Then the pinks and maroons from their teens, and the blues and lavenders from their twenties. Nobody wore kimonos anymore, except on special holidays. Her daughter Aya sometimes sent her modern clothing—white blouses and pale blue or even maroon skirts—and asked her not to wear her gray and brown kimonos anymore; they made her look so old. Masa continued to wear her kimonos. She *was* an old woman, she reasoned, and old women did not wear blues and maroons—no more than men wore pinks and reds, although young people now seemed less concerned about such distinctions.

As she tightened the mottled gray sash around her kimono, Masa thought of Yuki, who had visited her for two weeks during spring break. Together, they had sown the early seeds in the garden: peas and spinach, radishes, pansies. One afternoon, Yuki went through the old kimonos Masa had saved in the attic from her younger days. "You wouldn't want to wear those," Masa told her. "I don't know what I saved them for." They were not her best kimonos, which she had sold to buy food for her family after the War when they had lost their land and were poor. The kimonos in the attic were the cheaper ones she had worn from day to day. Most were damaged by moths and mildew. "If you don't mind my changing them or cutting them," Yuki said, "I would like to have a few of them. Maybe I'll use parts of them and sew something I can wear. My friend Isamu and I are going to learn to sew. We found someone to teach us. I didn't learn enough homemaking in high school." "You're welcome to the whole lot," Masa told her. "I'd have thrown them out a long time ago if I had ever gotten around to cleaning the attic." Though she laughed at Yuki's wanting such old useless things, she had been pleased. With her latest letter, Yuki sent a picture of herself wearing a quilted vest she had made from the kimonos. "What do you think?" she had written on the back. "I hope you don't mind my cutting them up so much. I wanted to wear the same things you did, only in a different way." Masa didn't mind at all. She was touched. Yuki would come for another two-week visit in June. "Can I invite a friend just for a few days while I'm there?" she had asked on the phone. "I want him to meet you and see where I grew up. He's my best friend." She paused. "He's also my boyfriend," she said. "You'll like him." "Of course," Masa said. "It will be good to see him." After they hung up, though, she felt sad that Shizuko and Takeo would never be able to meet any boy Yuki went with. Even the things that brought her happiness, Masa thought, made her sad.

Masa put the futon in the corner of the room and went to the kitchen. It was already the end of May, but on entering the kitchen she felt the chill. Because she no longer cooked a great deal, her kitchen was always cold. Shivering a little, she put rice and beans on the stove and waited for her daughter-in-law, Etsuko, who would drop by with her older son, Tadashi. For the last year, Etsuko had been working every other day at a factory in a nearby city, sewing cheap clothing, and Masa took care of Tadashi, who was four. There was a room at the factory where the children could play, and a woman was hired to watch over them. Etsuko left her younger boy there, but Tadashi sulked all day and got into fights with the other children. After he gave one boy a black eye, Etsuko was asked not to bring him back. Tadashi didn't take much to anyone except his parents. As far as Masa could see, Yuki was the only person he seemed to like from the first time he saw her. On her last visit, he had followed her around the garden. They went to the small stream in the back of the house to watch the catfish swimming. Once, they even waded into the mud, "to see if the fish would swim over our feet," Yuki said. They had come back with their toes caked with mud and laughing.

When the food was ready, Masa brought the tray from the altar. She cleaned up the cups, filled them with the freshly cooked rice, beans, and tea. She carried the tray back to the altar, lit two incense sticks, and bowed her head.

Before her thoughts formed into a prayer, the front door rattled. Masa left the incense burning and went to answer. Smiling and brisk, Etsuko nudged Tadashi into the doorway. His eyelids looked puffy.

"Please make sure he takes a nap," Etsuko said. She was carrying the younger boy, Tsutomu, on her back. "He didn't sleep well last night. It's getting so humid in the house."

"I don't want to take a nap," Tadashi said.

Etsuko momentarily tightened her grasp on his shoulder and then said to Masa, "My husband tells me to pick you up after work and bring you home. It's your birthday, isn't it? We want to have you over to dinner."

"That's kind of you and Saburo."

"I should be here around five. I'd better go now."

Etsuko drove off and, as usual, Tadashi spent the first half hour sulking. Masa left him on the threshold, where he sat drawing on the ground with broken twigs. Once in a while, he lifted his foot and rubbed out the pictures with his shoe. Masa ate her breakfast and cleaned up the kitchen. Tadashi had refused to eat with her ever since he had found a dead fly in the corner of her cupboard. Etsuko permitted him to bring his own box lunch, which he ate with his own chopsticks brought from home in a plastic case, and a thermos of weak tea, which he drank out of a plastic cup attached to the lid. It was as well. Masa no longer ate lunch herself.

After her breakfast, Masa worked in the garden. There were dead leaves to be snipped off her spring chrysanthemums, weeds to be pulled. Tadashi sat by the hedge and caught tiny tree frogs in a mayonnaise jar. That was what he did nearly every morning they were outside. It didn't matter how many times Masa explained that the frogs would suffocate inside the jar. Day after day, Tadashi would go home with a jar full of dying frogs.

"Why don't you help me pull these weeds?" Masa said.

"That's boring." Tadashi grimaced.

"You can make it less boring by pretending. The weeds are enemy soldiers and you can behead them, like this." Masa pulled a handful to show him. "And while you're doing that, I have to go to the shed and get more sticks for the peas to climb onto. They're getting tall now." She walked away, seeing the child slowly move toward the flower bed.

Inside the shed, before her eyes adjusted to the dimness, Masa almost stumbled over the bench that was once placed under the persimmon tree. Takeo used to sit on the bench after his evening bath to point out the constellations to the grandchildren. He told them the story of the two stars separated by the Milky Way, how they came close in July and then were pulled apart again, night after night. In the fall, when the grandchildren had gone back to their cities, Masa and Takeo would sit on the bench under the sky studded with persimmons and talk late into night. Now, everyone was grown up except for Tadashi and Tsutomu, who scarcely remembered Takeo.

A garden snake crossed her path, thin and gray like her sash. Masa took a few of the bamboo branches left against the wall and walked away.

When she returned to the garden, Tadashi was sitting

between a small heap of weeds and another small heap of white chrysanthemums. He shook the mayonnaise jar to make the frogs jump.

"Why did you snip off the flowers?" Masa asked.

"They died fighting the enemy soldiers," Tadashi said.

Masa did not know whether to laugh or scold. She seldom scolded. All the same, children and grandchildren alike had always taken to Takeo, who knew exactly when to scold and when to be amused. She finished putting up the sticks for the peas, while Tadashi dug a hole in the corner of the garden to bury the dead of his flower-weed war. If he buries them deep enough, she thought, the weeds won't come back up.

The noon siren went off in the distance while Tadashi sat on the steps and ate his lunch. Masa was crouching several feet away over her lantern flowers. Something was eating their leaves, but she couldn't see what. The tight buds were a darker purple than the flowers.

"Mama's just getting off for lunch now, isn't she?" Tadashi asked.

"She must be," Masa said.

"She said there are *hundreds* of sewing machines. Are there? Where she works?"

"I guess there are."

"I know there are. I saw them in my dreams. Needles came out of them like bullets." Tadashi had put down his chopsticks and was squinting into the sunshine.

"Is that why you can't sleep? You have bad dreams?"

Tadashi took up his chopsticks and stuffed his mouth with rice, yanked at a bit of chicken. Between mouthfuls, he said, "No. I can't sleep because it's too hot."

After he had finished his lunch, Masa took him inside

the house. On the sun porch, Tadashi stopped and looked at the wooden slide.

"You can play on the slide for a while before you take your nap," Masa said.

"No," Tadashi said. "I don't want to get splinters."

"You won't get any splinters. See how smooth it is." Masa ran her hand down the wooden surface.

"I'm too big for it," Tadashi said.

Masa could remember the day Takeo had finished the slide, two weeks after Shizuko was born. Built for young children, the slide had only five steps. All of her children and grandchildren had played on it over the years. She could remember Tadashi climbing it and sliding down continuously on the day of Takeo's funeral, while they were waiting for the priest to arrive. When the priest came to chant and the coffin was opened for the last viewing, Tadashi howled until Yuki brought him outside and walked around the garden with him. For months, Tadashi said that his grandfather was stuffed in a large trunk in the attic. When you asked him to play on the slide, he said that it had splinters, that it would break.

Tadashi ran his hand tentatively down the slide. He still held the mayonnaise jar in his other hand. The five frogs in it were immobile.

"Do you find any splinters?" Masa asked.

He shook his head.

"Let me hold your jar while you climb up and slide down, just once."

"It'll break," Tadashi said. "I'm too heavy."

"Not if you put down the jar. Your father played on this slide until he was much bigger than you."

Tadashi hesitated.

"Go on," Masa insisted. "You're not scared, are you?"

That did it. He thrust the jar into her face and cautiously climbed up the five steps. As he sat on the top with his legs stretched, he looked at Masa, hard, before he let go. It only took a moment before he was on the floor, scrambling to his feet. Without a word, he snatched the jar from Masa's hand. His jaw was set hard.

"Well, it didn't break and you didn't get any splinters," Masa said.

Tadashi walked ahead of her into the family room, still without speaking. Masa handed him a blanket and a pillow. He lay down on the floor, his back to the altar, and put the jar of frogs by the pillow.

"Do you want me to read to you, or are you already sleepy?"

Tadashi just closed his eyes. To Masa's relief, he was asleep in less than five minutes. His mouth, so often distorted sullenly while he was awake, relaxed in his sleep and his face was flushed from the morning in the sun. Inside the mayonnaise jar, one of the frogs made a feeble attempt to jump. It made a faint noise against the glass.

Why should I let them die? Masa thought. She took the jar in her hand. Tadashi might cry when he found out that his frogs were gone. Still, someone had to teach him not to kill, not even such small, insignificant creatures.

Masa took the jar out into the garden. She held it upside down and set the frogs free by the peony bushes. The frogs stayed limp and immobile for a minute and then, one by one, they disappeared among the green leaves and buds. As she dropped the empty jar in the waste bin by the house, Masa caught sight of something white on the window screen. She went closer to see.

It was a cicada, newly out of its shell. Its body and wings were still white, wet, shiny like waxwork. Masa found the brown, cast-off shell on the ground. With its protruding eyes and crooked legs, the shell looked alive except for the crack in the middle. Her boys used to collect them. Takeo used to tell them how the cicada spent seven years underground before it could fly and make droning noises among the tree branches, how it was more patient than any other creature on earth. But the cicada on her window screen looked as though it might be dying, so white and waxlike. After the seven long years, Masa thought, the birds will get at it.

Masa snipped off a peony leaf and put the cicada on it. It was wet and cool, a little slippery to the touch. She walked back to the house and went to the family room. Tadashi was still sleeping. Masa put the peony leaf and the cicada on the altar and sat down. The cicada did not move. If it's going to die anyway, she thought, it might as well die here, where Takeo can see I have offered it to him, the first cicada this summer. The incense sticks from the morning had burned to the bottom and crumbled, leaving a trace of fine gray dust. Masa closed her eyes and thought of Takeo and Shizuko.

It's my birthday, I'm seventy-five, and all I can think of is your death, she thought. A few years ago, crying would have relieved the dull pain in her chest, but tears seemed to have dried up in her after Takeo's death. I'm a woman deserted by her husband and her daughter, she thought. I want to join you soon, she said to them; I pray to you and to the spirits of our ancestors to take me to you. Let me join you in peace.

Imagining that her prayer might be answered if only she could remain still with her eyes closed, she moved away from the altar and lay down next to Tadashi. She was tired. His regular breathing lulled her. As she fell asleep, Masa thought of Shizuko driving all the way from the city to see her. It was Masa's birthday, and Shizuko had brought her pink and white peonies and a kimono of silvery gray that she had sewn for her. The peonies, larger than her face and so pale, kept nodding, brushing against her cheeks, and she felt her daughter dressing her in layer after layer of soft silk, silver and gray. Like a cocoon, Masa thought, endless folds of silk.

After what seemed like a long time, Masa heard a faint droning from far away. The noise grew louder, faded, and came back even louder. Masa opened her eyes and saw that Tadashi was not in the room. Slowly, she rose and walked to the sun porch, in the direction of the noise. There, she saw the child running up the steps and sliding down the wooden incline in quick repetition, in an almost frenzied circle of movement. For a split second, it seemed as though there was not one but many children—all her children and grandchildren going down the slide, one by one, laughing and chattering. Then it was Tadashi again, and the cicada flying in circles in the porch over his head.

Tadashi, going down the slide, raised his arms. "See the cicada, cicada, cicada. And no splinters on the slide. No splinters, no splinters," he chanted.

Masa walked to the window and pulled it open. Immediately, the cicada flew out and swirled up, merging into the blue sky. Masa stood by the open window and watched the child still running up the steps and going down the slide. She laughed, and cried copious tears, until her chest and shoulders ached from joy.

Notes on the Setting

This novel takes place in Japan, whose four major islands are Hokkaido, Honshu (the main island), Shikoku, and Kyushu. Most of the chapters are set in Kobe, a city on the main island, about four hours southwest of Tokyo by the express "bullet" train. Along with its neighbor Osaka, Kobe is one of the major industrial and cultural centers of Japan. Like many large cities in Japan, Kobe developed as a port town on a narrow strip of land between the mountains and the Inland Sea.

Himeji, another city mentioned in the novel, is also in the southwestern part of the main island. It is a much smaller city, however, and the area around it is rural: rice paddies, timber forests, rivers, and small villages scattered among them. Though the actual distance between Kobe and the countryside around Himeji is much shorter than the distance between Kobe and Tokyo, travel to the countryside would take several hours because the trains and buses that go there are fewer and slower.

Nagasaki, the setting of some of the later chapters, is on the southernmost island, Kyushu. Developed as one of the first Japanese port towns in the sixteenth century, Nagasaki is also a major city, but the area around it is mostly agricultural. It would be a long day's journey by rail (on trains that go through an underground tunnel between the islands) from Nagasaki to any of the cities in the Kobe-Osaka area.

Another thing to note about the setting—aside from the geographical references—is the Japanese school year. While the American school year consists of two semesters of roughly equal length, the Japanese school year has three terms of varying length. The year, which begins in April and ends in March, is divided up this way: the first term starts in early April and ends in late June. After a two-month summer vacation, the second term is from early September to late December. Then after a two-week winter vacation, the third term goes from early January to mid-March. Students stay in the same grade from April until the following March. As in the United States, students go to six years of elementary school and six years of secondary school (three years of junior high school and three years of high school). At the end of their last year in high school, students take entrance examinations to get into colleges of their choice.

Glossary

Chapter Three

Page 19. Kyoto, a city famous for its historical sites (old temples, shrines, palaces), is about an hour from Kobe on the commuter trains.

Page 21. Land reform: After World War II, the occupation government in Japan attempted two reforms meant to aid the rebuilding of the country's economy. One was to break up the financial conglomerates, which monopolized the industries (and also had manufactured weapons during the War); the other was to redistribute the land on which people cultivated rice, the major agricultural crop of Japan. While the first reform never succeeded, the second made major changes in the countryside. Before the War in the rice-growing villages throughout Japan, one or two families owned all the paddies and rented them out to others, who worked as their tenant farmers. Though the tenant farmers performed the actual task of cultivating the rice, they had to pay a large portion of their crops to the landowning families as rent and were very poor. In the process of the land reform, the landowning families were required by a special ordinance to sell their paddies to the government for very little money. They were allowed to keep only a small portion they could cultivate on their own. The government then distributed the newly acquired paddies to the tenant farmers. While the reform increased productivity among the former tenants (because, as predicted, people were more willing to work hard on land they owned rather than rented), many landowning families felt that the reform was unfair because they lost the land that had belonged to them for generations. Most landowning families were reduced to sudden poverty.

Chapter Four

Page 27. Futon: a Japanese-style bedding or mattress. It is often folded up and stored in the closet during the daytime so the room has more space. A typical Japanese house in a city would have both the traditional straw-mat (tatami) rooms, where people sleep on futons, and "Western" wood-floor rooms, where people sleep on beds. Houses in the countryside, on the other hand, tend to have only the traditional straw-mat rooms.

Page 31. Pottery villages: In the mountains north of Kobe are small villages where people make pottery. A typical pottery village would consist of several multigenerational families that own kilns. Almost everybody in the family would learn and perform some part of the pottery making, such as preparing the clay; forming the clay on potters' wheels; glazing, painting, or drawing on the pots; or firing the kiln. People who collect pottery often visit these small villages.

Chapter Five

Page 43. Because the novel takes place in Japan, the distances for the athletic events are in metric units. The race Yuki runs—1,000 meters—is approximately 1,100 yards.

Chapter Nine

Page 102. Tempura is a traditional Japanese method of preparing vegetables, seafood, and meats by cutting them into small pieces, dipping them in a flour-and-egg batter, and deep-frying them.

Chapter Fourteen

Page 172. Haori jackets were traditionally worn with kimonos. Today, older people often wear them over their Western-style clothes.

Acknowledgments

Earlier versions of the following chapters were previously published:

"Housebound," "The Wake," and "Tiptoes" as "Yuki" in *Maryland Review*, Fall 1988/Spring 1989, Vol. 3, No. 1.

"Pink Trumpets" in Florida State University's *Sun Dog: The South-East Review*, Summer 1985, Vol. 6, No. 2.

"Yellow Mittens and Early Violets" in *The Forbidden Stitch: An Asian American Women's Anthology*, edited by Shirley Geok-lin Lim and Mayumi Tsutakawa. Copyright © 1989, Calyx Books.

"Grievances" in *Crosscurrents*, 1991, Vol. 10, No. 1.

"Homemaking" in *Prairie Schooner*, Summer 1992, Vol. 66, No. 2.

"Winter Sky" in *The Kenyon Review—New Series*, Fall 1991, Vol. 13, No. 4.

"Epilogue" as "The First Cicada" in *The Apulachee Quarterly*, 1982, No. 18.

ONE BIRD
by Kyoko Mori

When her mother is forced to take a sudden and mysterious trip, fifteen-year-old Megumi must live alone with her father (who is never around) and her grandmother (who is unfortunately always around). Just when she begins to feel that no one cares, Megumi meets Dr. Mizutani, a veterinarian who offers her a part-time job healing sick birds. Her new job offers Megumi a chance to heal her wounds and rebuild her life and her family.

Published by Fawcett Books.
Available in bookstores everywhere.